THE TRIO
OF
MAYAVAN

Hema Yanamala

Clever Fox®
PUBLISHING

Chennai • Bangalore

CLEVER FOX PUBLISHING
Chennai, India

Published by CLEVER FOX PUBLISHING 2025

ISBN: 978-93-6707-799-3

Chapter 1

"Ansh, wake up!" shouted Samira, stepping into her son's room. Her eyes scanned the mess, scattered toys and clothes dumped across the floor. As she walked in, her foot slipped on a few colourful marbles hidden under the rug. She stumbled, caught the wall for support, and sighed.

"We're cleaning your room today. You must learn to stay organized," she said firmly.

"But Mamma, my summer holidays just started! I think you've forgotten that," Ansh laughed, stretching lazily. "I want to enjoy every bit of it. I promised my friends Amir, Zayan, Menorah, and Riya that we'd have an adventurous day today. We're known as the 'Fabulous Five' at school. We always have the best time together!" His eyes sparkled with excitement as he spoke of his friends.

"No, Ansh. Not today," Samira said sternly. "I want you to get ready and have your breakfast and remember that we are cleaning your room today . We're leaving for Mayavan, your grandparents' place in a couple of days. It's been far too long since we visited them."

"But Mamma," Ansh protested, rubbing his eyes, "I don't want to miss out on the fun with my friends."

"I understand," Samira said more gently. "We've missed so many chances to go because of our busy schedules. But I promise you'll have a wonderful time in Mayavan. Your grandparents love you deeply and miss you terribly. Think about it. I don't want to force you."

After breakfast, Samira and Ansh began tidying up his room, a task that took quite some time. Once done, Ansh went out to meet his friends. They sat under their favourite tree, chatting away.

"I'm not sure if I should go," Ansh said uncertainly. "We had so many plans for this summer."

"Why don't you give it a try?" Menorah suggested reassuringly. "It's only for a short while."

"It might even be fun!" added Amir.

"You can tell us all about it once you're back," said Zayan.

"We'll miss you," said Riya softly, and the group huddled together in a warm hug.

After spending a little more time with his friends, Ansh returned home. Post lunch, his thoughts lingered on their conversation and his grandparents. A wave of nostalgia washed over him, and before he knew it, he had drifted off to sleep.

Later that evening, he woke to the sound of his parents chatting on the balcony. Ansh joined them, his mother with her tea and his father, Raghav, gazing at the glowing sunset.

Ansh hugged his mother and said with a smile, "I'm really looking forward to going to Mayavan now."

"I'm so glad you've changed your mind," said Raghav, pleased. "You're going to have a wonderful time."

The three of them talked for a while and then headed out for dinner at Ansh's favourite restaurant. By the time they returned, Ansh was so tired that he went straight to bed and fell into a deep, peaceful sleep.

Meanwhile, in the village of Mayavan...

"Please, Mamma," begged Rudra, eyes wide with curiosity. "I want to know what's behind that old wooden door. Is it a treasure? Or something magical? What's the secret?"

"No, Rudra," Veena replied gently. "You're not supposed to go near it. The time hasn't come yet. You must wait a little longer." She stroked his hair and smiled. "You will be accompanied soon on your quest. That door only reveals itself to those who are truly destined and of the lineage."

"There's so much I want to know," Rudra murmured. "Where am I going? Why me? And who will go with me?"

"All in time," Veena said with a soft smile. "You'll learn everything on your journey."

Still restless, Rudra turned to his favourite hobby, painting. He tried to push the old wooden door from his mind and focused instead on the lively scenes in front of him.

A vibrant bird pecked at nuts on a branch while a pair of squirrels quarrelled and darted between tree holes. He began sketching the picture of a monkey swinging from vines, leaves rustling in motion. His drawing felt so vivid, it almost looked real. He placed the painting carefully on the mantel to dry.

Later, Rudra wandered to the nearby lake. Sitting by its calm waters, he lost himself in thought, grateful for the memories he had made in that peaceful place. Everything had been normal until the day he first saw the door in their garden. He had run to tell his mother, and to his surprise, she hadn't dismissed. Instead, Veena had looked astonished. She hugged him tightly and whispered, "You are destined to see it, Rudra. Not everyone can."

That moment changed everything. Since then, Rudra had waited eagerly for the day the door would open. And now that his mother had told him it would be soon, his heart brimmed with excitement.

As he collected pebbles by the lake, a gentle voice called out, "Hey champ, I knew I'd find you here."

It was his father, Praneet, who joined him with a smile. Placing a comforting hand around Rudra's shoulder, he said, "You know, I've never seen any door in our garden. But your mother mentioned something after you were born. She wondered if you were like her, destined."

He paused thoughtfully. "I never pressed her for answers. I knew she'd tell us when the time was right."

Rudra lay his head in his father's lap, comforted by the steady rhythm of the breeze and the sound of birds in the trees. After a while, they headed home for lunch, their bond strengthened by quiet understanding.

Elsewhere, in a hidden realm...

An emergency meeting was underway. The council had gathered in urgency, voices heavy with concern. Their once safe haven was now threatened by a dark force lurking in the shadows.

"I saw a woman across the river," someone spoke with a trembling voice. "She vanished into thin air before I could reach her."

"My neighbour was attacked," said another. "She barely escaped with her life."

Fear rippled through the crowd as they each recounted the strange and terrifying events they'd faced. One speaker nearly fainted from the memory.

"This place isn't safe anymore," someone whispered. The murmur spread like wildfire until voices rose in panic.

"We cannot stay here!" many cried.

"But where would we go?" others asked.

Just then, a commanding voice rang out above the chaos. "Calm down, everyone!"

Silence fell like a blanket as all eyes turned to the leader.

"This is our home," the leader declared. "And we will protect it. Peace must be restored, not through fear, but through unity."

Heads bowed in respect. The leader continued, "We are intelligent beings with strength and honour. The events of late are troubling, yes, but we are not helpless. If we stay united, we can defeat any darkness that threatens our land."

The crowd, inspired and steadied, began to disperse.

Once they were gone, the leader turned to the inner circle of council members. "Now," the leader said gravely, "we must decide how to face what lies ahead."

***

Chapter 2

Ansh woke to the cheerful sound of birds chirping. He stretched lazily and drew back the curtains, allowing the sun's rays to spill into his room. The soft light painted the space in hues of orange and pink, creating a warm and inviting glow. He noticed a few birds perched on the windowsill and rushed downstairs to grab some grains from the kitchen to feed them.

"Good morning, Ansh!" Raghav greeted warmly. "Be careful while running down the stairs," he added with a smile. "Slow down and watch your step."

Ansh winked and replied cheekily, "I'll always follow your advice, Papa!" Then, he darted into the kitchen, returning with a handful of grains for the eager birds.

As the morning progressed, the family busied themselves preparing for the journey.

Ansh reminded Samira to pack his favourite snacks while he carefully selected a few cherished books to bring along. Samira did a final check of every corner of the house, ensuring everything was in order, before locking up.

Once on the road, Ansh gazed out of the car window, watching buildings and trees blur as they sped past. Though he felt a pang of sadness about leaving his friends behind, the excitement of the trip to Mayavan kept him distracted.

The weather was perfect, pleasantly warm with a cool breeze that danced through the air. “Papa, can we lower the windows for a while? I love this weather!” Ansh asked eagerly.

Raghav nodded, “I love it too,” as he rolled down the windows. The family relished the fresh air, chatting and laughing, until a loud thudding sound startled them. The car came to an abrupt halt.

“What was that?” Samira exclaimed as all three stepped out to investigate. They found a large tree branch blocking the road. Relief washed over them that it hadn’t fallen on their car.

Ansh looked at his parents with a mix of curiosity and concern. “Papa, who’s going to help us move this? The road is empty!”

Raghav placed a reassuring hand on his son’s shoulder. “We’ll have to manage it ourselves. There’s no use waiting for someone else to come along.”

Ansh smiled confidently. “We make a great team!” Samira joined in, and together, they worked to move the branch. After a few tiring attempts, their combined effort paid off, and the path was clear.

“Unity is our strength!” Ansh cheered triumphantly.

Back in the car, Ansh started reading one of his favourite stories and heard faint voices as if someone was calling him for help but couldn't find anyone around as they were travelling and in the middle of long journey ahead. He had familiar experience on few occasions in his house while playing in his garden, while going to school, but, didn't give much thought to it.

He mentioned this with his mother and she assured him that everything is fine and there is time for everything and things will go as destined. He even noticed her making a few phone calls in her room after their conversation they had on the fainted voices. He couldn't understand anything but kept quite not to give her any additional stress. This time too he brushed it off but soon dozed off, lulled by the rhythmic hum of the car and the refreshing breeze.

He woke up as darkness fell and found himself at a cosy roadside eatery. The family enjoyed a hearty meal, with Ansh feeling refreshed and energized from his nap.

After dinner, Raghav pointed to the sky, where airplanes were descending towards a nearby airport. He parked the car by the highway so Ansh could watch the planes land. Fascinated by the sight, Ansh couldn't tear his eyes away, excitedly chatting about each plane's graceful descent. Ansh cheerfully said that getting on and off the plane is different but watching the Flight land from outside is a new experience.

Later, with their spirits high, Ansh selected his favourite playlist, and the family spent the remainder of the drive singing, laughing, and enjoying each other's company. It was a perfect escape from their daily routine. Samira was glad that Ansh consented to the trip and they had the best time spent on their journey.

Meanwhile, in Mayavan Village...

Rudra sat restlessly, his thoughts racing. He felt a strange pull, as though his destined companion for the mysterious quest was near. Unable to contain his excitement, he went to Veena.

"You can sense their presence, can't you?" Veena said, her voice calm yet knowing. "I've always known you had this gift, Rudra. It's a blessing."

Feeling comforted, Rudra brought his canvas into the backyard and began to sketch.

After sketching Monkey's realistic picture which turned out to be beautiful, he started to sketch another picture to calm down his thoughts.

This time, his imagination brought to life a magical creature, a unicorn. He painted its spiralling golden horn, its pristine white body accented with soft pink and purple streaks. As he stepped back to admire his work, Praneet appeared, smiling.

"It's beautiful," Praneet said, pointing to the unicorn. "But doesn't it need a tail?"

Rudra laughed and realized his oversight. He moved to correct it, but his father stopped him. "Leave it as it is," Praneet suggested. "It looks perfect. Why not draw another one instead?"

Encouraged, Rudra started a second painting, pouring even more attention into the details. When he finished, both pictures looked stunning. Proud of his work, he carefully rolled them up along with an earlier drawing of a monkey, storing them safely in a corner of his room.

Later, Rudra joined his parents in the garden, where they sat on a swing sipping coffee. They chatted about everything under the sun, the cool breeze and serene surroundings adding to the tranquil mood. Veena felt blessed to have such a loving family and she was very proud of Rudra, but hid her feelings so as not to give unnecessary thoughts to anyone around her.

"Rudra, your school sent your grades," Praneet announced, holding up his phone. The results were impressive, and the family decided to celebrate.

On their way back from visiting Rudra's teachers, they stopped at a cosy restaurant nestled near the woods. The place was enchanting, with oil lanterns hanging from trees, casting colourful patterns through stained glass. Tiny birdhouses dotted the branches, and a clear stream flowed nearby, its soothing sounds blending harmoniously with the environment.

"This restaurant was opened by a dear friend," Praneet said, smiling. "He wanted people to experience nature at its best."

Veena nodded in agreement. "It's free from noise and pollution. Truly a hidden gem."

The family enjoyed a delicious meal served on banana leaves and earthenware, marvelling at the eco-friendly setup. As they ate, Praneet revealed the restaurant's true origins. It was his idea, inspired by Veena's love for nature. He had worked with his friend Vignesh to make it a reality, keeping it a secret as a surprise. Veena didn't know how to respond. Rudra hugged his father and thanked him for the lovely surprise.

Staff members clapped and brought out a cake for Rudra to cut. As they celebrated, Veena's eyes welled with tears of joy. "This is the best gift ever," she said, feeling blessed by her family's thoughtfulness. She couldn't ask for more.

Praneet then announced that Veena would take charge of managing the restaurant, fulfilling her dream of creating a space that celebrated nature.

In the Mysterious Place...

The caretakers were deep in discussion about their next steps. "Should we summon the 'Trio'?" one asked. "We cannot face the evil alone."

"It's been years since a 'Protector' entered our land," another said. "Only they can restore balance, as they have in the past." But the things happening now are most dangerous compared to the earlier incidents, said another.

The council debated fiercely, some arguing that their powers alone were enough, while others expressed doubt, wondering why the Guardians always needed to protect them. The leader finally spoke, his voice calm yet authoritative.

"Our powers are immense, but this evil spell binds us. Even combined, we cannot break it. Only a true protector, someone destined and pure can free us. We must guide them, but their courage and intelligence will lead the way. Our ancestors assigned specified powers and tasks for each and every person and their families carry on the legacy through generations and we must abide by them." Protectors are one such important kind which must be carried out with lineage and not by choice but by the destiny they were being chosen and must be respected.

The leader's words silenced the dissent. The council dispersed, their spirits lifted by the hope of the Protectors arrival, ready to embrace the golden days ahead when the 'Trio' would fulfil their destiny.

***

Chapter 3

It was early morning by the time Ansh's family reached the village of Mayavan.

"We'll be at your grandfather's house in just a few minutes," Raghav said, stretching his arms as he drove through the village roads. The sight was a pleasant to the eyes as trees formed a canopy above with birds tweeting and flying from one tree to another. The sounds of the birds were enchanting mixed with cool refreshing air coming from the nearby lake soothing the soul and everything felt amazing.

Houses are small but beautiful and people are greeting each other on their way. Everything seemed amazing to Ansh. He started to notice the difference from the hustle – bustle life in his city and the calmness in the village.

Ansh, wide-eyed and alert despite the long journey, gazed in awe at the rising sun. "There's nothing more beautiful than this," he murmured.

"The golden rays painting the clouds, the sunbeams piercing gently through the tree branches and touching the earth, it feels like the world is slowly waking up to a magical beginning."

The car finally pulled into the familiar driveway, and as the sound of the engine reached the house, Ansh's grandparents rushed outside. His grandfather enveloped him in a tight, warm hug, and Ansh melted into his arms.

Only a day ago, he had been reluctant to come. But now, standing in his grandfather's embrace, he felt something shift deep inside. *This*, he thought, *might just be the best holiday ever.*

Ansh's grandmother greeted Samira with a big smile and hugged her tightly. Watching them, Ansh chuckled and winked at Raghav. "Look, Dad! Mamma is happiest when she's with her mamma."

Raghav laughed and said, "Come on, let's all go inside and catch up."

They stepped into the cosy house, weary from the journey but comforted by the familiar sights and smells. Refreshments were served, and soon after, Ansh, Raghav, and Samira took a hot bath to freshen up.

As Ansh and his father sat in the living room admiring the greenery outside, Samira helped her mother in the kitchen. Before long, Raghav and Ansh joined them to lend a hand and lighten the workload.

Later, Krishna, Ansh's grandfather, suggested they all visit the fields for some fresh air. However, Samira and her mother decided to first visit some relatives and planned to meet them at the field later. So Krishna, Raghav, and Ansh headed out together.

Ansh was mesmerized. The lush green fields, especially during the growing season, stood out vividly against the natural landscape. A gentle breeze rustled the crops, creating a rhythmic swaying that filled the air with calm. The earthy scent, the openness of the fields, and the vibrant hues brought a deep sense of connection, something Ansh hadn't expected. It was altogether a new experience for him. He wondered how he had missed such beauty all these years.

After some time, Samira and her mother joined them. As they walked, Samira called someone on the phone. Curious, Ansh asked, "Mamma, who was that?"

She smiled. "A friend for life."

Ansh grinned. "I hope I find a friend for life here in Mayavan, too."

Samira smiled and said, "We'd better walk faster, or we'll be left behind."

"Mamma," Ansh said thoughtfully, "isn't that what we always do, running through life in a rat race? We keep chasing things, thinking we're getting closer, but sometimes we forget to enjoy the journey. Let's slow down and enjoy this walk."

Samira stopped in her tracks and looked at him with wide eyes. Gently pulling him closer, she ruffled his hair. "Big boy Ansh," she said softly, "I didn't realize you'd grown up so much. You're right. I'll follow your advice and live better."

They walked together, slowly, enjoying the breeze and the birdsong.

"You're going to meet someone very special soon," Samira said mysteriously. "You'll make memories that will last a lifetime. You'll go on a quest together."

Ansh turned to her, puzzled. "A quest? What do you mean?"

"You'll find out soon," she replied, winking. "Don't stress over it."

Suddenly, Ansh froze. "Mamma," he whispered, "I think someone's been watching us... I saw a tall figure. I'm afraid to look."

Samira followed his gaze, and upon seeing the figure, smiled mischievously. "Close your eyes and trust me," she said, holding his hand.

They walked toward the figure and stopped. "Now open your eyes."

Nervously, Ansh opened one eye, then both of them and burst into laughter. Standing before him was a scarecrow. It was stuffed with dry grass for the body, typically made to resemble a person, wearing a pot for head supported by stick fixed firmly in the ground for posture and painted features to enhance the illusion.

"That's a scarecrow," Samira explained, grinning. "It's placed in fields to scare off birds and animals so they won't eat the crops. They will be made in different forms creatively making different types of them, some usually wearing a hat or a cloth tied into turban and wearing different types of old clothes (dhoti/trousers and a shirt) resembling a person. When you see one, it usually means we are in a farm ."

"Wow!" exclaimed Ansh. "I've seen scarecrows at Halloween parties, but never like this. I didn't know what they were actually for. I learned something new today!"

Suddenly, a rhythmic drumming sound echoed nearby. Ansh turned to see a man holding a steel tin and a thick wooden stick, beating the tin to create the loud noise.

"It's another way to scare off birds and animals," Samira explained. "There are many such traditional methods."

Samira began showing Ansh more methods farmers use to protect crops from natural repellents to clever field techniques. Ansh was fascinated. Everything was new, and every moment felt like a learning adventure.

Eager to learn more, he rushed to his grandfather with questions, determined to make up for lost time and cherish every bit of this trip. He promised himself to visit Mayavan more often and to bring his grandparents the joy they always gave him.

Meanwhile, in another part of the mystic world...

A tall, shadowy figure stood amidst swirling dark energy. His voice roared through the silence, filled with fury.

"You couldn't even drop a tree in the right place?" he shouted, his eyes glowing red.

His trembling disciples bowed low. "Master... we calculated everything and tried implementing it, but a speeding car came out of nowhere and overtook the target vehicle, slowing it down. The branch fell too early."

The dark figure clenched his fists, teeth grinding. "They're being protected again," he growled. "They are shielding the chosen ones with their powers... but this isn't over. If they won't heed my warnings, they will suffer."

The disciples quivered in fear, hoping they wouldn't be punished. But the dark figure suddenly changed tone.

"You must be more careful. One day, you will be my ministers when I rule as King."

A flicker of relief passed across the disciples' faces.

But it was short-lived.

Without warning, the dark figure raised his wand, whispered a command, and hurled it into the air. The wand spun, glowing with malevolent energy, and began striking the disciples one by one. They cried out in pain, begging him to stop.

With another sharp chant, the wand returned to his hand.

"Let this be your final warning," he hissed. "Fail again... and the consequences will be far worse."

The disciples, panting and shaken, bowed deeply and promised themselves they would never fail again.

***

Chapter 4

Ansh was tired and hungry by the time they finished exploring the vast, lush green fields. He had spent hours asking his grandfather endless questions about everything around them. His grandfather, patient and affectionate, answered every one of them with a smile, cherishing these moments he had longed for all these years.

It was almost afternoon and everyone were hungry. Somu, their loyal servant, arrived carrying lunch from home. He was accompanied by Aadya, Ansh's cousin, who lived with their grandparents. Aadya had lost both her parents in an accident, and since then, the grandparents had lovingly raised her. When Aadya greeted Ansh, his grandfather introduced her as a distant cousin.

They began unpacking the lunch basket when Ansh suddenly exclaimed, "Oh no! We don't have any plates. How are we going to eat?"

His grandfather chuckled, turned to Somu, and said, "Go cut a few fresh banana leaves." Then he turned to Ansh and smiled, "These are our beautiful, natural plates, gifts from Mother Nature."

Soon, all of them sat cross-legged on a mat under the cool shade of a wide, ancient mango tree. Lunch was served on the vibrant green banana leaves, still fresh and moist from the tree.

"This is amazing!" said Ansh as he took a bite. "Food tastes so much better on these leaves. And it's even more special because I'm eating with all of you."

This was a whole new experience for Ansh, and he loved every bit of it.

Aadya, cheerful and talkative, started chatting with Ansh about the village. "I've seen you in photos," she said, "and your grandparents talk about you all the time. You should visit more often. They have missed you terribly."

Ansh smiled, nodding as he listened to Aadya tell stories about her friends, the local fair, and the village life. He realized he had not only found a cousin but also a wonderful new friend.

As the sun began to lower in the sky, their grandfather stood and said, "Time to head home."

That evening, back at the house, Samira spoke to Ansh about her best friend, Veena.

"You'll be going to her house tomorrow," she said. "She has a son named Rudra and he's about your age. I really hope you two become great friends, just like Veena and I."

"Rudra?" Ansh repeated, surprised. "Mamma, I think I know that name. I can barely remember, but I think I've played with him before. It's like a blurry memory from when I was little."

Samira smiled warmly. "That's right. You both used to play together as toddlers. But as time passed, our visits to Mayavan became less frequent. My parents couldn't travel often anymore; the city was too much for them. And with your father and me caught up in our busy schedules, we barely found time for anyone. We kept in touch only by phone, which is what kept your grandparents going."

Ansh felt a wave of guilt wash over him. He realized that relationships, whether with family or friends require time, effort, and presence. When neglected, they fade quietly until it's too late to fix them.

He made a silent promise to himself: *I will never again let distance grow between me and the people I love.*

Wanting to shake off the heaviness in his heart, Ansh asked, "Mamma, can Aadya come with me tomorrow? I think she'll enjoy it too."

Samira smiled. "Of course! That's a lovely idea." Your journey will be incomplete without Rudra and Aadya.

Ansh pressed her for more information, she smiled and said that he will get to know everything tomorrow.

When Samira told Aadya about the plan, she lit up with excitement. "I'd love to come! I've seen Rudra a few times and met his mother. She's very sweet."

Ansh, still curious about Rudra, said, "I have vague memories… I'm excited but a little nervous."

Aadya winked. "You'll know everything tomorrow. Don't spoil the suspense, life is boring without a little mystery."

Ansh laughed. "Ha-ha, you're funny!"

Both of them shared a hearty laugh before heading off to their rooms. Ansh lay in bed thinking about the adventures tomorrow might bring, and with a smile on his face, drifted into a deep, peaceful sleep.

Aadya dreamt about a mysterious hidden land with nature so beautiful that she had never come across in real life. She always used to have this dream but, now, the place seemed to be gloomy. She couldn't understand anything as it was a dream and didn't give much thought to it.

In the Mystic World...

In a hidden realm untouched by time, the leader stood tall before the caretakers and council members.

"I want to commend you all," he said solemnly, "for protecting 'The TRIO', not once, but on multiple occasions."

There was a murmur of gratitude in the crowd.

"You saved the boy when the tree branch fell near their vehicle," he continued. "And again, in the field, when the scarecrow was tampered with to cause harm. You also prevented the other protector from being abducted by the enemy when he sat near the river."

Everything was taken care of except saving the family of one person belonging to TRIO. But, still, we managed to save her.

The crowd listened intently.

"And let us not forget," the leader added, "how you intervened when the boy was lured by the injured bird near his school in Mayavan village. It was a trap. Had he attempted to return the bird to its nest, he would have entered the danger zone, an illusion designed by dark forces. Thanks to his teacher's timely warning and your silent guidance, he went home safely."

The leader's tone grew firm. "They are our Guardians, but until their powers awaken, we must protect them. Even if it costs us everything, our duty is to ensure their safety. This is the responsibility each of us must carry with honour."

A silent vow passed through the room, an unspoken promise of loyalty and sacrifice, as they prepared for what lay ahead.

Chapter 5

Ansh woke up early, brimming with excitement. He quickly got ready, and Aadya joined him right on time. Krishna, Ansh's grandfather accompanied them up to the outskirts of the village, where they arrived at a breathtakingly beautiful house nestled in the lap of nature.

It was a serene sight, the house stood gracefully surrounded by vibrant flowering plants and tall trees with aerial roots reaching toward the earth. The trees swayed gently in the breeze, as if nodding in welcome. Flower petals floated down like nature's confetti, forming a delicate carpet beneath their feet. A cool breeze from a nearby stream embraced them like a warm hug, while distant hills framed the view like a painting.

They walked slowly, taking in every detail, their eyes wide with wonder. Eventually, they reached a grand wooden door carved with intricate designs, each curve and symbol etched with precision and purpose. Ansh lifted the brass knocker and gave it a gentle knock.

The door opened almost immediately. Standing there was a boy with a kind smile, sharp eyes, and neatly groomed hair. Ansh couldn't help but notice a dark mole on his right palm, shaped uncannily like a butterfly tattoo.

"Welcome," said Rudra warmly. He was nearly the same height as Ansh and greeted Aadya cheerfully. "My mom told me you were coming. I've been looking forward to meeting you."

Inside, Rudra's mother, Veena, greeted them with joyful surprise. She embraced Ansh and said, "I'm your mom's best friend. Samira and me were inseparable growing up. We used to sneak out of our houses to play, getting into all kinds of mischief."

As she spoke, she served them delicious snacks and natural fruit juice made from fresh fruits plucked right from their backyard trees.

"I always wished for you and Rudra to be close," Veena added. "But time and different routines kept that from happening. I have always wanted to stay close to Aadya but couldn't due to various reasons. Maybe that's about to change."

Veena showed them around the house, which was open, airy, and surrounded by life. Birds chirped in every corner, sunlight filtered through large windows, and the scent of flowers filled the air.

Ansh was enchanted. "I've never seen a home like this," he said, in awe. "It's like living in a forest dream."

Then, as they walked near the garden fountain, they came upon a small, weathered wooden door, half-hidden by cascading water and lush greenery. It looked ancient.

Ansh and Aadya stared at the door. Rudra caught their gaze, smiled knowingly, and said, "I've always wondered what lies behind that door, too. But my mother says the time isn't right yet."

He turned to Veena. "Are Ansh and Aadya the ones you spoke of? The ones who'll join me on the journey?"

Veena nodded, her eyes twinkling. "Yes, Rudra. The time has come."

Rudra's eyes sparkled with excitement. "Can we know the truth about the door now?"

Ansh and Aadya nodded eagerly.

Veena took a deep breath. "Many years ago, Samira, Leela (Aadya's Mother), and I went on a mystical journey together. Before us, our fathers—Nandan, Krishna, and Shyam were the first 'Trio' of our lineage to enter the magical world of 'MAYAVAN Kingdom' after we had come to the real world away from our motherland to protect it from outside invaders. This legacy has been passed down for generations. Each trio has had a different mission to fulfil."

She paused, her gaze distant with memories. "Your grandfather Nandan always said that the adventure must remain a secret until the next generation is ready. And now, it's your turn."

Ansh listened with wide eyes as Veena continued.

"Nandan believed that each mission would be unique, and that each protector must discover their own strength. Help will come, but you must also rely on each other. Just as we did. You will cherish the journey, no matter the challenges."

She then dialled a number and walked to the balcony, scattering grains for the birds as she waited. Turning to the children, she smiled.

"There's a magical world behind that door. You'll find mystical beings, challenges, and enchantments beyond imagination. I was waiting for Ansh to come… and now Aadya is here too. The new Trio has formed."

Just then, the doorbell rang.

It was Samira.

The moment Veena opened the door, the two old friends stood speechless, tears brimming in their eyes. "It's been almost a decade," whispered Veena.

They embraced tightly. No words were needed. Though they had spoken often on the phone, meeting in person after so long was overwhelming. They missed Leela very badly. They wished she were here to witness the awesome journey of Aadya and also thought that she would be very proud of Aadya for being the destined one.

Rudra walked over with two glasses of water and gently placed his hand on their backs. Ansh sat beside them. "It's amazing," he said. "After all these years, you're still best friends. I hope Rudra and I can be the same."

"We will," Rudra said, with a smile. I am also a part of your tribe, stepped in Aadya. We are best friends for life and nothing can change this, the children said in chorus.

Ansh turned to Samira and began telling her everything.

She listened calmly and said, "I know. Veena and I have spoken. I trust you'll be careful. This journey will test your courage, but it will also bring you joy and wisdom. Be brave, and look out for each other."

"Thank you, Mamma," Ansh said. "I'm ready."

"So am I," said Aadya, with excitement.

Veena gave Rudra a lucky charm—a pendant with a bold "V" engraved on it.

"Is it for your name?" Rudra asked.

Veena smiled. "Maybe. Or maybe it's something more. You'll know when the time comes."

Meanwhile… in the Mystic World

"I can sense it," growled the dark figure, his cloak swirling in the dim light. "The *Trio* is arriving. We must prepare."

His disciples trembled. One of them spoke hesitantly, "Master… perhaps we should not fight them. The people of the mystic world have always been kind… perhaps we should—"

"SILENCE!" the dark figure roared. His eyes glowed crimson with fury. "After everything I've done for you, your food, shelter, protection, you DARE speak of kindness?" You have to be grateful for everything I gave you. Instead, you are taking their side, he growled.

He began to pace, restless. His desire to become the ruler of the mystic world and eventually, of all worlds gnawed at his mind. But the arrival of the Trio unsettled him.

Still, he tried to rationalize.

They see me as the villain… but I am the true saviour. I must show them my power.

He took a deep breath, calming his nerves. "No one can defeat me. I am invincible. The Trio will not succeed. I will never let that happen." I am the strongest, and nothing can change this.

But deep down, the shadow of doubt lingered and his false pride blinded that very thought.

***

Chapter 6

Veena led the children near the fountain, where the ancient wooden door stood silently behind a curtain of greenery, waiting patiently for the right time to open. She knelt beside the fountain and removed a patch of grass from behind it, revealing two hidden valves.

With practiced hands, she rotated one valve clockwise and the other counter clockwise—three full turns each. Suddenly, a magnificent peacock figurine rose from the ground. Its wings spread wide in a dazzling display, gleaming with gold and encrusted with radiant gemstones that shimmered under the sunlight. The colourful stones glinted brilliantly, and the feathers fanned out as though the peacock were ready to perform a magical dance.

The entire space sparkled with reflections from the gemstones, casting prismatic patterns across the area.

Veena carefully placed marble-sized stones, each one identical in size and weight on the feathers on one side of the figurine. Samira mirrored her movements on the opposite side. Slowly, the peacock figurine sank into the earth, and with a soft rumble, the old wooden door began to lift.... slowly, steadily, as if welcoming the children to explore the depths of the magical forest.

Veena gave a gentle nod, signalling the children to enter.

Rudra, Ansh, and Aadya stepped through the doorway, their eyes wide and filled with wonder. The door began to close quietly behind them.

"Bye, Mamma!" Rudra called out. "I love you. See you soon!"

Ansh glanced at the closing door and said with a grin, "I thought there would be a key to open it."

Rudra chuckled. "You can't expect a key to open a magical forest!"

Aadya giggled and nodded in agreement.

They turned around and stood in awe. The forest stretched out before them, a breath-taking spectacle of nature's grandeur. Towering trees loomed above, their ancient trunks wrapped in vines and moss. Birds chirped from hidden branches, and golden rays of sunlight pierced the canopy above, dancing between leaves and casting warm beams on the mossy forest floor. Though the trees were thick and old, the sun fought through stubbornly, sending down shafts of light like gentle spotlights.

The ground beneath them was soft, blanketed in lush moss like a green carpet rolled out just for them. In the distance, the soothing sound of a waterfall echoed through the woods, its melody calming their hearts and minds.

Rudra climbed onto a low-hanging branch that swayed gently like a swing, enjoying the breeze and the peaceful view. Ansh lay on his back, gazing up through the thick canopy at the glimpses of blue sky. Aadya closed her eyes, swaying slightly, listening to the harmony of birdsong, quietly humming along.

Each of them soaked in the moment in their own way.

"We should continue," Rudra said eventually, hopping off the branch. "There's still so much to explore."

Ansh sat up. "Do we know what we're supposed to do? I remember Aunt Veena saying there's a mission."

"We'll find out," Rudra replied. "I think the forest will show us the way. Let's enjoy the journey and stay open to whatever comes."

The three friends began walking. As they moved forward, something remarkable happened. The path before them began to widen, as if the forest itself was responding to their presence, clearing the way. The trees gently bowed, vines retracted, and the mossy path stretched out before them like a living guide.

"Is it just me," Aadya whispered, "or is the forest… helping us?"

"It definitely is," Ansh replied, eyes wide. "This is incredible."

Then, Rudra suddenly raised a hand. "Shh… did you hear that?"

A tiny voice echoed faintly from the trees ahead.

Rudra motioned for silence and pointed toward the direction of the sound. The children stepped quietly, following the faint voice, but no one was in sight.

Looking around, Rudra's eyes landed on a monkey perched on a tree branch, munching on a bunch of bananas.

"Rudra!" Ansh whispered, pointing. "That monkey looks exactly like the one you painted!"

Rudra and Aadya exchanged stunned glances, astonished at the resemblance.

Just as they were about to move on, the monkey looked up, set down his bananas, and spoke.

"Today is the day," said the monkey in a gentle voice. "I've been waiting for you. Finally, you're here."

The children froze, eyes wide, momentarily speechless.

"You… you can talk?" Ansh asked, still trying to comprehend what he just witnessed.

"Yes," the monkey replied with a chuckle. "And I've been expecting you."

Rudra stepped forward, cautious but curious. "How do you know who we are?"

"All your questions will be answered in time," the monkey replied. "For now, just know this: I am your guide. You may not need me always, but when you do, I'll be there."

He held out a small bunch of bananas. "You're not hungry now, but take these. They'll come in handy during your journey. It's still a long way ahead."

The children gratefully accepted the fruit.

With wide smiles and hearts full of wonder, they thanked the talking monkey and continued deeper into the enchanted forest unaware of the challenges that awaited, but braver for the magical encounter that had just unfolded.

***

Chapter 7

The monkey handed Rudra a map of the forest and said gently, "This will guide you through the forest. If you ever feel lost or need help, just call my name."

Rudra, realizing their oversight, apologized. "We were so overwhelmed, we forgot to ask your name."

The monkey pointed to the map, where a name was beautifully etched in curling script: Hanu.

The children smiled and thanked Hanu again for the map and his help. "We'll definitely come meet you again," Aadya promised.

The wind carried earthy scents mixed with the fragrance of wildflowers, a hint of moss, animal musk, and wood. Aadya closed her eyes and inhaled deeply. "Wow! Such a beautiful blend of smells... it's like the entire forest is alive."

The trio waved goodbye to Hanu and resumed their journey. As they walked, the path widened before them, as if the forest itself was welcoming them. Trees swayed gently, nodding their branches in greeting, while bright green grass blanketed the earth. Massive moss-covered stones dotted the landscape, and here the sunlight filtered more freely, falling in golden shafts through the gaps in the canopy.

The rustle of leaves beneath their feet, the whistle of the wind, and the symphony of chirping birds blended into a music they had never heard before, a melody of the forest itself.

"It's… overwhelming," Rudra said softly. "The scents, the scenery, everything feels like it's telling a story."

Ansh, normally talkative, was speechless. His eyes shone with wonder.

Just then, a gentle voice came from behind, interrupting their awe.

"Hello, Trio. I hope you've found help and are settling in well."

The children turned around, startled. Standing behind them was a tall, radiant woman who looked like she had stepped out of a fairy tale. She smiled warmly, her presence both regal and nurturing.

She wore a velvet green dress, soft as grass, and on her head sat a magnificent crown adorned with green emeralds and delicate wildflowers—bluebells, cornflowers, borage, vetch, and more. At the centre of the crown rested a large oval emerald, positioned at her forehead like a third eye—the green eye, protector of nature.

A long, flowing robe of emerald silk glittered faintly in the sunlight, its golden accents forming intricate patterns as she moved. Her hair, braided and adorned with vines and tiny flowers, shimmered with vitality. Her eyes were wide and compassionate, filled with a deep, ancient wisdom. The children immediately felt calm and safe in her presence.

"I am Princess Dhatri," she said, her voice smooth and serene. "The green fairy, protector of this forest. No one enters without my knowledge. I guard it fiercely from invaders. Hanu gives the map only to those who belong here… the True Guardians and that is what you are." The map automatically guides your path without having to look into it and it brought you here to me.

Rudra stepped forward, puzzled but intrigued. "But how do you know that we're the True Guardians?"

Dhatri nodded kindly. "True Seekers are chosen across generations. These powers, this connection, are passed down through your lineage. The magical door you entered? It appears only when the time is right and only to those who are destined. Even the correct placement of the peacock stones would not open it if the protector was not ready.

Ansh raised his hand hesitantly. "But… couldn't anyone place the right weights and open the door?"

"No," Dhatri replied gently. "The door remains invisible and immovable to anyone who is not a Protector. It responds to destiny, not science." There are many things in this universe that happens for a reason without the involvement of any math, physics, etc., and we call it 'Destiny'.

"So we really are the Guardians?" Rudra asked.

"Yes," Dhatri smiled. "Just as your mothers, Veena, Samira, and Leela, were the protectors before you. And before them, your grandfathers, Nandan, Krishna, and Shyam, walked the same path. There were many Guardians before you all who worked tirelessly to protect Mayavan and safeguard the subjects, and many who even sacrificed their lives for protecting their motherland. We always honour them and remember them.

Now, it is your turn. From today onward, it is the Trio that must carry the mission forward."

She turned to Rudra. "You, Rudra, will lead the group. Your sharp thinking and presence of mind will guide you well. Ansh, your intuition and skills will be crucial in moments of challenge. And Aadya, your intelligence and empathy will be your strength."

The three children exchanged looks of surprise and wonder.

Dhatri chuckled softly. "In time, you'll understand. But now, it's midday. You've walked far. Come, let us have lunch."

She led them through a series of natural arches, thick branches intertwined with vibrant blossoms in every colour imaginable. As they passed through, they reached a stunning structure. Its walls were made of firm yet soft white cotton, decorated with flowering creepers and tree branches that protruded through the emerald green canopy above. Shiny gemstones hung from the ceiling like chandeliers, and each room entrance was marked by unique arrangements of precious stones instead of doors.

Inside, the rooms were spacious. Large enough to fit ten people comfortably. Beds made of pure silk offered comfort like nothing the children had ever experienced. Tables and chairs had been sculpted naturally by intertwining tree limbs.

Dhatri led them to their respective rooms. They were enchanted but also very hungry. Soon, they gathered in the grand dining room, where green-dressed helper fairies served an enormous spread of delicacies. The fairies were little more than the size of butterflies. Their wings are exquisite and felt like shiny transparent glass. They are busy bringing in the dishes with their little hands and carefully placing them on the table. Later on, they rushed fast but carefully, not to bump into each other and make a mess. The dishes were exotic, vibrant colours, delightful aromas, and flavours that danced on their tongues.

Aadya admired everything around her and thanked the little fairies for everything they had done.

Rudra closed his eyes in appreciation. "I can taste the essence of forest in this meal."

Dhatri beamed. "Anything for our Guardians. You are part of us now."

After the meal, Dhatri suggested them to rest. "There's much more to see. But for now, sleep. You've had a long day."

The children returned to their rooms, falling into a deep, peaceful sleep. When they awoke in the evening, they were served hot herbal tea, fresh, fragrant, and healing. Rudra sipped it and sighed, "Even the tea tastes like a blessing."

That night, the helper fairies guided them through a trail that led to a clearing among massive trees. At first, it was dark, so dark they could barely see. But then...

A gigantic light show unfolded.

Thousands of fireflies lit up the clearing, their glowing bodies flickering in unison. They soared above the children like living stars, creating sparkling patterns across the sky. It was as though the night itself had come alive in a dance of light.

The children stood in silence, their faces glowing with amazement.

Eventually, they returned to the dining room for a light dinner. Before retiring for the night, Rudra turned to Dhatri. "Thank you. For everything… especially the amazing fireflies show."

Ansh and Aadya echoed their gratitude.

"You are welcome, my children," Dhatri said softly. "This is only the beginning."

That night, the Trio drifted to sleep, their hearts full of wonder and their minds swirling with dreams of magic, fireflies, and the secrets still waiting to be uncovered in the enchanted forest.

***

Chapter 8

Rudra woke to a soft, glowing morning. The sun played hide and seek through the thick branches of ancient trees, casting dappled light on the forest floor. He stretched, took a deep breath of the fresh woodland air, and made his way to meet Dhatri, the green fairy.

She greeted him with her usual warm smile. "Good morning, Rudra."

As they sat beneath a canopy of emerald leaves, Dhatri's tone turned serious. "There are rare moments," she began, "when the fairies lose their power, only for a few minutes. But in those brief moments, darkness creeps in. Evil uses those powerless seconds to cast invisible spells, to tamper with the balance we protect. By the time we regain our strength, the spell has already been woven. Everything appears normal on the surface, but beneath it… something begins to rot."

Rudra listened intently, eyes wide.

"These cursed spots," Dhatri continued, "are later used by dark forces to break into our world. That's when the Guardians are needed, when the enchanted forest calls for help."

She gently took his hand, touching the charm his mother had given him. "You are one of the chosen ones, Rudra. I cannot tell you everything now. But when the time is right, you will learn from the right person. Until then, trust yourself. You have what it takes. You're not alone."

Her reassuring smile filled Rudra with newfound confidence.

Later, Dhatri led the children to a serene, crystal-clear lake. Its waters shimmered in the morning light, revealing fish gliding through coral gardens and vibrant aquatic plants swaying gently below the surface. The lake was encircled by neatly trimmed lawns and topiary trees shaped like animals, stars, and mythical creatures.

She guided Rudra down a hidden stone staircase behind the lake. Ansh and Aadya followed silently. At the bottom, they found a giant, circular, velvet-green cushion embedded in the earth.

"This," said Dhatri, "is the next phase of your mission. You'll meet new allies… and perhaps some challenges. But do not be afraid. Step forward, Rudra."

Without hesitation, Rudra stepped onto the cushion and vanished.

Ansh and Aadya quickly followed, disappearing into the unknown.

Rudra landed gently on a massive maroon mushroom, its cap springy and soft. Looking up, he saw Aadya and Ansh landing on similar mushrooms nearby. All around them were enormous mushrooms…. red, pink, and maroon, towering like trees, with tiny glowing mushrooms nestled between them like stars dotting the forest floor.

The place felt dreamlike. Everything was unusually vibrant, and the trees were adorned with red and pink blossoms that looked too perfect to be real. Ansh reached out to touch a flower. It felt like crinkled paper.

Suddenly, a mysterious voice echoed around them: **"Watch out… because you are being watched."**

Startled, Rudra jumped up and signalled for his friends to stay close. He cautiously moved toward the direction of the sound. There, hidden behind a mushroom, stood two strange figures—dwarfs, wearing long black shirts, golden trousers, and tall pointed hats. Their white beards nearly touched their waists, and their eyes glinted with mischief, or perhaps malice.

"Who are you?" Rudra asked.

But without a word, the dwarfs vanished.

Just then, a soft voice called out, "Rudra, Ansh, Aadya—welcome."

A graceful woman emerged from between the trees. She wore a crown of flowers and leaves, and her robe shimmered with the colours of blooming petals. "I am Princess Rosa, fairy of Flora and guardian of the beauty in this part of the forest. You are now in the land of Rosa and Aruni."

The children smiled with relief, but Rosa's tone turned stern for a moment. "You must not go near the half-destroyed wall beyond those trees. It is dangerous and cursed. Promise me you'll stay away."

Rudra opened his mouth to explain what had happened when they arrived, but before he could speak, a loud, angry voice interrupted them.

"Stop being so welcoming, Rosa!"

A stern woman with sharp eyes stepped forward. "I don't trust outsiders in our land. They always bring trouble. I don't see why we should need the help of the so-called 'TRIO' – The

Guardians. Why should we need help from those who left Mayavan to save it, instead of staying and protecting it from within?" She rolled her eyes angrily.

Rosa sighed and said softly, "This is my sister, Aruni, the protector of this realm. Don't mind her. She speaks from pain, not cruelty."

But Aruni had already turned and disappeared into the forest, her flowing robe vanishing behind a wall of pink leaves.

The children stood silent, feeling a little shaken and unwelcome.

"We promise," Rudra finally said. "We'll stay away from the destroyed wall."

Aadya and Ansh nodded, still processing the encounter.

They wanted to ask Rosa about the mysterious dwarfs, but held back, unsure whether it was the right time.

Rosa smiled gently. "Don't worry, Trio. Everything will work in your favour."

Though her voice was calm, she looked thoughtful as she turned away. In her heart, she knew what had truly happened when the children arrived… and she didn't want to burden them, not yet.

"They will know everything when the time is right," she whispered to herself, watching the Trio disappear into the forest's heart.

✻✻✻

Chapter 9

Meanwhile, Akku and Tikku, the two dwarfs who had earlier threatened the children, hurried into a dark, damp cave. They stood silently with their heads bowed low before their master.

"The Trio has arrived," they murmured.

A deep, echoing laugh filled the cave. Sitting on a stone throne was Kaal— a gigantic man with a cruel expression and a malicious grin, his broad, muscular frame wrapped in dark robes. His long, matted hair was tied neatly into a high bun, and in one hand, he held a dark sceptre that crackled faintly with energy.

"So..." he growled, voice like thunder. "They've arrived. That means they've learnt that I am too strong to be defeated and more powerful than everyone in Mayavan and therefore brought the Guardians inside the forest from their hideout place."

The Princesses of Mayavan are confined to their realms helplessly and the day Mayavan comes under my control, they will become my servants forever. Let them enjoy their freedom now as I have the most important task of bringing Mayavan under my control. Once it is done, everything becomes easy.

No protector can defeat me. I will write their destiny. They have come a long way to meet their end in my hands. He leaned forward, his eyes glowing. "Let the hunt begin. We will not lose, never."

Kaal rose and walked toward a large crystal ball placed on a stone pedestal. He closed his eyes, chanted an incantation, and waved his sceptre over the ball. The cloudy surface shimmered and cleared, revealing Rudra, Ansh, and Aadya chasing butterflies and hopping like rabbits, giggling in innocent joy.

Kaal roared with laughter. "These children think they can defeat me?"

Akku cautiously stepped forward. "Master… the Trio has always been the true Guardians of Mayavan. They've saved it every time, with loyalty and unmatched strength. They must not be underestimated." They are born with the immense power destined to protect their motherland.

Kaal's expression darkened. "I could have ended one of those boys the day I disguised myself as a scarecrow in the field, but his mother saved him."

Akku trembled. "Master… what about Princess Dhatri, the Green Fairy? She will protect them with all her power."

Kaal sneered. "She can protect them, but she cannot harm me. She knows that. Her power is only for protection, not destruction."

"I will destroy the Trio," Kaal declared. "Before they understand the extent of their power. Before they even know what they are truly capable of."

Tikku, ever the sycophant, quickly chimed in, "Master is all-powerful! We believe in you! Don't listen to Akku—he only brings doubt."

Akku protested, "But we must speak the truth. Blind praise leads only to ruin. I speak for your safety, Master."

"Silence!" Kaal's voice boomed. "You dare question me?"

With a wave of his hand, he ordered, "Tikku, don't give him food and water. Let him starve and hang him upside down before the furnace until he learns his place!"

"Please, Master!" Akku begged. "I only meant to protect you!"

But Kaal turned away, unmoved.

"You shouldn't talk to our master that way, Akku. His anger will bring you more trouble. Face the consequences", said Tikku sadly.

Back in the land of Rosa and Aruni, Ansh was deep in thought, recalling all the strange events that had happened so far. "We still don't know what exactly our mission is," he said.

"I spoke to Dhatri yesterday," Rudra shared. "She hinted that our real journey is only beginning."

"I'm starting to understand bits and pieces," Aadya added. "But we need more clarity. We can't help Mayavan unless we understand its past."

"Let's talk to Rosa," Rudra suggested. "She might have answers."

"Get set, go Trio!" Aadya cheered.

Laughing, the three friends headed toward Rosa's woodland cottage.

As they walked, a cheerful, familiar voice called out, "You're going the right way!"

"Hanu!" Rudra shouted with joy.

The monkey leapt in front of them with a wide grin. "I've been keeping an eye on you to make sure you're safe."

He led them to a crystal-clear river, its waters sparkling in the morning light. The atmosphere was so calm, it felt like stepping into a dream.

"I could live here forever," sighed Aadya. "It's like serenity has a home."

With a snap of his fingers, Hanu summoned wooden chairs for the children. Ansh laughed and said, "I want to sit on the branch with you, Hanu!"

With another snap, Ansh was magically seated on a high branch beside him.

"You're a real magician!" he said in amazement.

"You haven't seen anything yet," Hanu grinned. "Are you ready for a surprise?"

He clapped his hands, and the riverbank transformed into a forest theatre with a glowing stage. Hanu made swirling gestures in the air. Suddenly, a talking crocodile appeared in front of them.

“Welcome, dear guests!” said the crocodile. “I am your host for today’s show.”

Aadya giggled, “You should wear a sparkly jacket, hold a mic, and wear shades to look cool!”

“Right away!” said the crocodile.

He spun in a blur and transformed. He now wore a glittering outfit, a wide-brimmed hat, sunglasses, and held a shining microphone. The stage lit up with colourful disco lights, shimmering laser beams, and floating orbs of light.

“Let the show begin!” they all shouted together.

The show opened with a dance performance by multicoloured fish, twirling and flipping in sync to lively music. The giraffe played piano, the cheetah strummed a guitar, the lion beat the drums, and the birds chirped the chorus, led by a melodious cuckoo.

The choreography was mesmerizing. Fishes formed patterns, created waves, and danced to every beat with perfection.

Next came two graceful unicorns, playing violin and harp. The music was beyond words, haunting, beautiful, and pure.

Aadya's eyes widened. "They look like the unicorns Rudra drew!"

Rudra nodded in awe. "It's exactly them…"

The performance came to a magical close, and with a final snap, everything vanished, returning the children to the forest path.

Hanu led them along a steep trail, pebbles crunching underfoot, until they reached a stunning cottage nestled beside a large lake. Peacocks danced, elephants trumpeted, and deer pranced playfully behind the bushes.

The cottage was surrounded by natural fountains, shimmering waterfalls, and colourful water flowers blooming in every shade imaginable.

Everything was painted in soothing hues of blue, calming their racing thoughts and inviting peace into their hearts.

Where are we going? Asked Ansh. The way to Rosa's woodland cottage is the other way round as it is shown in the map.

Hanu said that it was just their stop for a while before entering the main step for their mission.

Chapter 10

Rudra pointed toward a graceful woman dressed in flowing blue robes, her crown adorned with sparkling sapphires and delicate chains of tiny diamonds cascading from its centre to her forehead. Her long hair was neatly braided and intricately decorated with shimmering strands. She stood by the lake, feeding royal swans with dandelion petals and lettuce leaves.

"She must be Princess Neeli," Rudra whispered. "The Blue Fairy… the protector of water bodies and aquatic creatures."

Neeli noticed them and gently signalled Hanu to bring the children to her. Hanu nodded and led them forward. As Neeli began to speak, her voice was soft as velvet, melodious like birdsong, enchanting the children instantly.

Rudra gave a respectful bow. "Your Grace, we seek to know about our mission."

Neeli smiled kindly. "To understand the present, we must first delve into the past," she said. Her tone turned serious as she continued. "Only then will you comprehend what lies ahead."

Aadya stepped forward. "Please, Princess Neeli… we would be grateful if you could tell us the history. We want to understand why we're here and what must be done."

Neeli's eyes shimmered as she looked toward the sky. She began weaving a story that transported them into the past, painting vivid pictures with her words:

"There was a time when our homeland, Mayavan, was a realm of peace and harmony, where diverse beings lived together like one united family. It was a land filled with joy, love, and an unshakable bond between its people.

My father, King Mayanand, ruled with compassion and wisdom. The people revered him, not out of fear, but out of deep respect and love. He treated every subject like his own child. My mother, Queen Maya, was just as beloved, nurturing, gentle, and graceful. Together, they ruled our beautiful Mayavan with fairness and heart.

We are five sisters, daughters of the king and queen. Though royalty, we were taught humility, service, and never to misuse our powers. We fulfilled our duties sincerely, and the people adored us for it. Mayavan flourished, abundant crops, limitless water, no poverty, no greed. It was a kingdom of smiles and serenity.

Each of us had a role to play. I, Neeli, am the second daughter. I oversee all the water bodies, rivers, lakes, rain, and aquatic life. My father taught me ancient spells to balance rainfall, prevent floods, and ensure water flowed where it was needed most.

My sister Dhatri, the third daughter, is the guardian of greenery. She cares for crops, trees, and all plant life. Using her magic, she can prevent outsiders from entering into Mayavan. She fertilizes lands and ensures bountiful harvests. Her connection with nature is unparalleled.

Then come the twins and the youngest among all of us, Rosa and Aruni. Rosa is calm and kind, the caretaker of flora and fauna, maintaining the forest's charm and restoring its beauty with her spells. Aruni, though fierier, is deeply loyal. She protects our land from outsiders and uses her magic to shield us from invaders. They've been inseparable since birth.

Together, we were happy.

But everything changed with the arrival of one man…"

Rudra, curious, interrupted gently. "Neeli… you haven't spoken about your eldest sister."

Neeli's expression shifted. Her smile faded. She averted her gaze, then softly said, "Let me continue…"

"A man named Kaal entered our lives. Tall, with sharp features and eyes that seemed always in search of something. He claimed to have no memory of his past, wandering in darkness, plagued by dreams he couldn't understand. He was sent by my father's teacher, Acharya Gopala, who said Kaal had lost his way and needed shelter.

Out of compassion, my father welcomed him into Mayavan. Kaal was respectful, humble, and helped everyone. He grew fond of nature and would spend hours in the forest, feeling at peace during the day. But by night, he was restless, haunted by his dreams.

Often, he would disappear into the dark woods, screaming in agony. Servants would search for him and bring him back the next morning. This became a routine. My father believed he would one day recover and even entrusted him with accompanying us on royal picnics and outings.

We, the sisters, admired his dedication and thought him trustworthy.

Then, one day… everything began to shift.

My father fell gravely ill. He realized his time might be short and wanted to ensure the kingdom's stability. So, after consulting our mother and elders, he made a decision, one that was to change our fate forever.

He chose to name his eldest daughter, our beloved sister as his successor…"

At that moment, Neeli's voice faltered. She paused, lowering her head. Her shoulders trembled as she closed her eyes tightly, as though trying to silence the flood of memories.

Aadya reached out and gently touched her shoulder.

A deep silence fell.

The children stepped back quietly, allowing Neeli a moment of peace. Even the animals grew still. The wind calmed. The trees stood frozen, leaves unmoving as if all of Mayavan were holding its breath, sharing Neeli's sorrow.

No one spoke. No one needed to.

The past had begun to unravel—and it was only the beginning.

Chapter 11

After a long silence, Neeli called the children and Hanu closer to her. Her eyes were distant, as though she were still lost in time. She pointed toward a distant, majestic mountain, its peak veiled slightly by mist.

"Such a huge mountain!" exclaimed Ansh. "Does it have something to do with your story?"

Neeli's voice turned firm. "It's not a story or folklore, Ansh. What I'm telling you is reality, a past that truly happened."

Rudra nudged Ansh with his elbow, and Ansh quickly apologized. Neeli softened. "It's alright. I let emotion carry my tone." I am sorry too.

"We know we're here for a mission," said Rudra, "but until you began telling us about your past, we were lost. Now… we want to help. We're ready."

Neeli nodded appreciatively and resumed telling about the past that changed their fate. .

"That mountain," she began, pointing again, "is called Pratham. It is sacred. Every important ritual begins there—births, ceremonies, celebrations. All of Mayavan believes that Pratham protects us from calamities and unseen dangers. It's more than a mountain…, it's our guardian."

Neeli paused for a moment, then continued with care.

"My father, King Mayanand, often visited the cave temple deep inside Pratham. After his prayers, he would always consult with his teacher, Acharya Gopala, a revered scholar, wise and compassionate. Acharya handled many of the kingdom's affairs. His guidance shaped Mayavan into what it was, a haven of peace."

Acharya Gopala wasn't only a counsellor; he was a master of many disciplines. He taught combat to the warriors, spells to Guardians and royals like us, and medicine, philosophy, and values to the common folk. Above all, he taught kindness and strength of character.

"One day," Neeli said slowly, "Acharya went into the forest with his disciples to gather herbs and roots for his lessons. As they moved through the undergrowth, they heard the faint moaning of someone in pain."

The children listened, wide-eyed.

"They rushed toward the sound and found a young man lying unconscious, bleeding from his head. His injuries suggested a violent ambush. Acharya quickly crushed a healing herb, rubbed it beneath the man's nose, and instructed his disciples to bring him to Pratham."

At Pratham, Acharya and his disciples worked tirelessly to treat the stranger. They ground herbs, bandaged his head, and monitored him day and night. King Mayanand, informed of the situation, visited the mountain and offered any aid required.

"Days turned into weeks. The man's condition stabilized. He began to move in his sleep. Then, one morning, he opened his eyes. Blank. Lost."

Acharya Gopala rushed to see him. The stranger was staring at the rising sun but said nothing. He drank the concoctions he was given but couldn't speak a word about who he was, not his name, not his past.

"He cried," Neeli said softly. "He held his head and sobbed, desperate to remember anything at all. But his mind was a blank slate."

Moved by the man's anguish, Acharya promised he would help. King Mayanand extended him a place in Mayavan. "You are one of us now," he said. "We will protect you."

The people agreed and welcomed him with warmth. There was some hesitation about naming him, but one bold voice requested Acharya to do the honour.

Acharya paused, then declared: "You shall be called Kaal." You will remember everything and stay victorious over time.

A cheer erupted. "Kaal! Welcome to Mayavan!"

The man, overwhelmed and speechless, nodded and bowed. He promised to serve the land that had embraced him and pledged undying loyalty to the king and to Acharya Gopala, whom he considered a second father.

In time, Kaal became a trusted member of the royal household. He was devoted, helpful, and respectful. He accompanied the royal family everywhere and remained close to Acharya.

"It all seemed too perfect," Neeli murmured. "And life rarely stays that way."

The children leaned in as her voice deepened.

"One day, Kaal wandered into the home of Bhushan, the personal assistant to Minister Mukund. He heard hushed voices.

Bhushan was negotiating with a stranger, but Kaal couldn't make out the words."

Curious, Kaal moved closer but accidentally knocked over a pot. The sudden noise alarmed Bhushan. The stranger, startled, fled through a hidden underground passage into the forest.

Bhushan rushed to the door, just in time to glimpse Kaal fleeing.

"Though Kaal hadn't heard anything," Neeli explained, "Bhushan believed he had heard *everything*."

Fearing exposure, Bhushan went straight to the palace, hoping to gauge whether Kaal had told anyone. But Kaal, genuinely shaken, had said nothing. He simply ran out of fear, fear of discovering something he wasn't meant to, or worse, being accused.

"But," Neeli said, her voice now tight, "that moment marked the beginning of the unravelling."

Kaal couldn't forget what he had seen or what he had almost heard. He grew restless again. Doubts began to fester in his heart. And Bhushan… Bhushan began to scheme.

The seeds of suspicion had been planted, both in Kaal and in others.

"And so," Neeli said with a heavy heart, "the harmony of Mayavan began to crack, unseen, unheard… yet unstoppable."

Chapter 12

Kaal couldn't sleep. As always, he wandered through the quiet forest, his thoughts circling back to the same burning question: Who am I? And, added to this ongoing situation, he was confused about what might have been going on with Bhushan. The unease wouldn't leave him.

Though he wanted to confide in King Mayanand about Bhushan, he held back. Without solid proof, he didn't want to create unnecessary conflict. He decided to quietly investigate, hoping to uncover the truth himself.

That night, Kaal slipped into the deeper woods, his heart heavy with more questions.

Meanwhile, in the shadows of Mayavan, Bhushan, cloaked in disguise, hurried through the underground passage. He had to meet the stranger again to warn him.

"Kaal might have heard everything," Bhushan whispered. "If he tells the king, we're finished."

The stranger, tall and grim, didn't respond at first. He stood silent, then finally turned and asked coldly, "Who is Kaal?

Bhushan told him everything about Kaal. You said this man, Kaal, entered Mayavan on the new moon?" asked the stranger. I think he had severe injuries all over, especially a grave injury on head, inquired the stranger.

Bhushan nodded. "Yes. What of it? And why are you suddenly so interested in his head injuries?"

The stranger's expression hardened. "He's not dead. You people.... you saved him."

His voice thundered through the narrow tunnel.

"You've ruined everything," he roared. "I will get rid of Pranav at any cost."

Bhushan reeled. "Pranav? Who is Pranav? Why do you want him dead?"

The stranger narrowed his eyes and replied slowly, "We both have the same goal, Bhushan, and it is to gain power. If we join hands, we can both get what we want."

Bhushan was confused. "I don't understand. Speak clearly."

The stranger sighed and removed his hood.

"My name is Kuldeep. I am a close associate of Prince Mahi Varma, the twin brother of Prince Pranav Varma, who is now living in your kingdom as Kaal."

Bhushan's jaw dropped. "Kaal? That refugee? He's royalty?"

Kuldeep clenched his fists. "Yes. And your people saved him. He was meant to die. I watched him fall. We thought it was over. But now... he's here."

Bhushan took a step back, the weight of everything beginning to sink in. "Now it makes sense. Mahi Varma always hated his brother. He feared Pranav would become king of Indraprastha."

Kuldeep nodded. "He's right to be afraid. Because everyone loves Pranav. Just like how your people respect King Mayanand. Mahi always believed the kingdom should be his alone."

Kuldeep continued.......

"Indra Varma, our King, was a just and noble ruler. He formed the Viswasith Sena, a trusted group of warriors who mingled among the people, gathering insights and ensuring harmony. No one knew who they were except the king and Minister Rana. Their reports kept our kingdom strong."

"When the queen, Ratna Prabha, died, she left behind her sons, Pranav and Mahi, as mere children. Our King raised them both with equal love. But Pranav mirrored the king in every way, gentle, wise, humble. The people adored him. And they feared Mahi's arrogance and cruelty."

Bhushan nodded in understanding. "Mahi was enraged when he learned that people didn't want him to rule."

"Yes," Kuldeep said grimly. "When he approached their father and demanded to be made heir, the king was shocked. He consulted with his ministers and the Viswasith Sena to gauge public opinion."

Bhushan interrupted. "But didn't Mahi find out about the meeting?"

"He did," Kuldeep confirmed. "He forced a palace guard to spy. The poor man feared Mahi's wrath more than the king's discipline. The guard overheard everything and ran straight to Mahi."

Kuldeep's eyes glowed with malice. "That was the final spark. Mahi was furious. 'Pranav Varma has turned the kingdom against me,' Mahi said. 'Now I will take what's mine.'"

"Mahi began plotting in secret," Kuldeep continued. "And that's when he heard about you, Bhushan."

Bhushan frowned. "Yes. I met one of his associates, Mahi Varma's envoy. We spoke about our shared ambitions. I always wanted to become king of Mayavan."

"You see?" Kuldeep sneered. "Both of us want power. And both of us are close enough to the royal courts to take it."

Bhushan fell silent. His heart raced.

Kuldeep watched him closely. "Now that we know Kaal is Pranav, we must act. If he regains his memories, everything will be lost. My plan failed once. It will not fail again."

Bhushan hesitated. "But… I still don't understand. Why didn't you tell Mahi earlier?"

Kuldeep's face darkened. "Because I was afraid. If Mahi finds out his brother is alive, he might kill me too, for failing. That's why we must finish what we started… together."

Bhushan stared into the darkness. "And if we don't…?"

"Then Pranav Varma will return. And everything we worked for, your throne, my freedom, everything will be gone."

Kuldeep paused, then added, "Remember, Bhushan. You were never meant to be loyal. You've always wanted more. I'm just showing you the path."

Bhushan didn't reply. Deep down, he knew what Kuldeep said was true. He had hidden behind a veil of service and loyalty, but all he ever wanted was power.

He clenched his fists.

"I'll think about it," he said, and turned to leave.

Kuldeep's final words echoed in the tunnel.

"You don't have long."

***

Chapter 13

Prince Mahi Varma didn't trust anyone, as he always feared that none could be trusted, even his own family or anyone who claimed to be his close associates. He dismissed the idea of collaborating with anyone, convinced that none could be relied upon. Instead, he devised a plan on his own.

Approaching his twin brother, Prince Pranav Varma, Mahi proposed a hunting trip to the nearby forest. Pranav, longing to mend the growing distance between them, eagerly agreed.

Mahi insisted that the outing be kept private, claiming it was an opportunity for the brothers to reconcile their differences. Pranav, trusting his brother, promised not to tell anyone.

The following morning, the brothers ventured into the forest, carrying bows, arrows, and just enough provisions for the day. They laughed and reminisced, sharing stories and enjoying the camaraderie.

As they rode deeper into the forest, Mahi subtly altered their path. When Pranav questioned the change, Mahi reassured him, claiming he had scouted the area earlier and discovered it was rich in wildlife.

Unbeknownst to Pranav, the altered route led them straight into an ambush. Suddenly, masked men emerged from the shadows, attacking Pranav from behind. He fell from his horse but quickly regained his footing, fighting back valiantly despite being unarmed, his sword missing from its scabbard. His brother Mahi is not there. He already trotted fast on his horse, nowhere to be seen. He left the place.

The realization struck Pranav like a dagger: his own brother had betrayed him. Overcome with shock and heartbreak, he hesitated, his defences faltering. The attackers delivered a crushing blow to the back of his head, and he collapsed. Believing him dead, the masked men carried his body deeper into the forest, where they abandoned him in the wild, expecting the beasts to finish what they had started.

Their leader, new to the forest and having already heard so much about it, assured that the Prince would not make it alive. He also admitted he didn't know exactly where they had left the prince, but assured the group it was a dangerous area no one dared to enter. The men, confident in their mission's success, quickly retreated.

Upon their return, the gang leader reported to Prince Mahi Varma, claiming that Pranav was dead and his body had been left for the animals. Mahi was relieved, convinced his path to the throne was now clear. That night, he celebrated lavishly, the weight of his brother's presence lifted from his shoulders.

The next morning, King Indra Varma summoned Mahi to the royal palace. Concerned about Pranav's unusual absence, the king demanded answers. Mahi, feigning guilt, crafted a story. He claimed that Pranav had expressed a desire to travel the world to better understand its people and governance. "He didn't want anyone to know," Mahi explained, "fearing they might stop him out of love or concern."

King Indra Varma, while saddened by the sudden departure, accepted Mahi's explanation. "If it is for the betterment of the kingdom, so be it," he sighed, praying for his son's safety. He praised Mahi for stepping up to manage royal duties in Pranav's absence. Mahi, relishing his father's newfound approval, promised to honour his brother's legacy.

However, fate had other plans. That very night, Acharya Gopala stumbled upon Pranav Varma in the depths of the forest. Barely alive, Pranav had no memory of who he was or where he came from. The wise teacher brought him to safety, nursing him back to health and naming him Kaal, unaware of his royal identity.

Back in the present, Neeli's voice trembled as she recounted these events. Tears, glistening like pearls, rolled down her cheeks. Aadya gently placed a hand on her shoulder, attempting to comfort her. Rudra and Ansh exchanged glances, their expressions a mixture of sympathy and determination.

"Neeli," Rudra ventured cautiously, "if Kaal, Prince Pranav… is truly good, why can't we simply speak to him and resolve the conflict?"

Aadya and Ansh nodded in agreement, hopeful that reconciliation could bring peace.

Neeli shook her head, her sorrow deepening. "The story is far from over," she said, her voice heavy with emotion. "What happened next sealed the fate of Mayavan and its people. To understand the danger we face, you must hear the rest."

The children listened intently, bracing themselves for the revelations yet to come.

***

Chapter 14

Dhatri descended gracefully from the sky, her magical wand gleaming in the morning sun. She landed beside Neeli and the children, her expression calm and serene. Though she had clearly been listening to their conversation from the beginning, she had chosen not to interrupt until now.

Rudra beamed with joy upon seeing her. He stood up, smiling, and offered a respectful salute. Aadya and Ansh joined him, their faces filled with curiosity.

Dhatri continued the story where Neeli had left off. "After Kaal was rescued and healed," she said, "he was fully restored in body, though not in memory. He was accepted by everyone in Mayavan and treated like one of their own. Kaal showed genuine respect, kindness, and gratitude to all, endearing himself deeply to the people."

"But everything changed when Bhushan, still suspicious, met Kuldeep from Indraprastha and falsely claimed Kaal had overheard a secret conversation. Without verifying the facts, Kuldeep took Bhushan to Prince Mahi Varma."

Mahi Varma, upon hearing the story, saw an opportunity. "I don't want to kill him," he said, "but I want to ruin his image and make him look like a villain in both Indraprastha and Mayavan so that I can be the best choice and Pranav would never be forgiven."

At the same time, in Mayavan, King Mayanand had grown increasingly impressed with Kaal, his bravery, battle skills, and noble conduct. The king was convinced Kaal came from royal blood and believed he could lead Mayavan with honour.

He went to his teacher, Acharya Gopala, to ask for his blessing to marry Kaal to his eldest daughter, Varna.

Acharya Gopala nodded thoughtfully. "You have my blessing," he said, "but beware.... challenges will come. They are tests of your nature, and they must be faced. The truth will be revealed in time. No one can escape destiny."

King Mayanand didn't press for more details. Instead, he consulted Queen Maya, though he didn't share Acharya Gopala's warning. He expressed his desire to see Kaal marry Varna.

Queen Maya smiled. "Kaal is brave, noble, and kind," she said. "He deserves our daughter."

Dhatri continued, "Our parents approached our eldest sister, Varna, and she happily agreed. She is a woman of compassion, always helping others without expectation. She saw in Kaal a reflection of her own heart."

"Can you tell us more about your elder sister now?" Ansh asked eagerly. "We haven't heard anything about her until now."

Dhatri smiled and gently touched the charm on Rudra's wrist, the one with the letter 'V' engraved on it. "My eldest sister," she said warmly, "is Princess Varna, a woman with a golden heart."

"Varna!" the children exclaimed in unison.

"We thought the 'V' stood for Veena, Rudra's mother," Aadya and Ansh added, laughing. Everyone joined in the laughter.

"She gave that charm to your mother," Dhatri said. "It is a symbol of pure love and affection showered on your mother as a token of appreciation. Veena became close to my sister's heart, a person whom she loved like her own. Varna never speaks ill of anyone. She forgives those who realize their mistakes. She is loved by all."

Neeli smiled and nodded in agreement.

"What happened next?" Rudra asked.

"My father called a council meeting," Dhatri continued, "and announced his decision to marry Varna to Kaal. Everyone agreed, except Minister Mukund, who was concerned about the implications. But my father reassured him. 'This is not just about the kingdom,' he said, 'but about my daughter's future and my faith in Kaal.' Eventually, Mukund agreed."

A grand celebration was held. Kaal was declared the future king and fiancé of Princess Varna. Invitations were sent far and wide. The people of Mayavan rejoiced, for they loved both Kaal and Varna dearly.

Acharya Gopala was given a seat of honour at the celebration, which was held in nature's embrace. King Mayanand introduced Kaal as his future son-in-law and king. Kaal and Varna took blessings from Acharya Gopala, and the people showered them with love and good wishes.

The celebration was full of joy, food, music, and unforgettable memories.

"But," Dhatri said softly, "danger was already creeping in."

"Time passed quickly," she went on. "Life returned to normal until Bhushan met Prince Mahi Varma through Kuldeep. He learned that Prince Pranav Varma, whom they believed to be dead, was alive and now set to become the king of Mayavan."

Mahi Varma was enraged. Furious that the gang had failed, he ordered their execution for misleading him.

Bhushan assured Mahi Varma he would handle everything this time. In return, he asked for Mahi's help in becoming the King of Mayavan. Mahi agreed but warned Bhushan of the dire consequences of failure.

Mahi said, "I don't want him dead. I want him disgraced, humiliated. Let him fall in everyone's eyes. He'll leave of his own accord, and no one will ever suspect us."

Bhushan smirked. "It's easy to appear good while making someone else look bad. Leave it to me."

***

Chapter 15

Meanwhile, in Mayavan, the entire kingdom was bustling with joy as preparations for the grand wedding of Princess Varna and Kaal, formerly Prince Pranav Varma, were in full swing. Though Kaal appeared elated, a shadow lingered in his heart. His forgotten past continued to haunt him, stirring an unsettling emptiness.

Varna sat beside him, sensing the turmoil behind his smile. "I understand what's going on in your mind," she said gently, taking his hand. "We'll find the answers soon. No matter what happens, I will always stand by your side."

Tears welled up in Kaal's eyes. He looked at her with deep gratitude. "I'm so lucky to have you in my life," he whispered. "And I will forever remain indebted to everyone in Mayavan, especially Acharya Gopala and King Mayanand."

Just then, Princess Varna's sisters, Dhatri, Neeli, Aruni, and Rosa joined them, playfully teasing, "Hope we're not interrupting anything important?"

Varna chuckled. "Not at all. We're family."

"A family," Kaal added with a smile, "is never a disturbance; it's everything."

Laughter filled the air, echoing with warmth and unity. In that moment, they all felt the strength of their bond and reassured one another that they would always have each other's backs.

Far from the celebration, Bhushan was deep in thought, plotting once more. He knew he couldn't kill Prince Pranav Varma but he could destroy his reputation. That, he believed, would be enough to have him exiled forever.

After much deliberation, Bhushan devised a scheme to frame Kaal as a traitor and a thief. He enlisted a group of thieves from a nearby forest and instructed them on how to breach the royal treasury. He even provided them with a detailed map of key landmarks, guard duty schedules, and a secret entrance behind the palace wall, an entry few dared to use, rumoured to be haunted and prowled by wild beasts.

That evening, as the sun dipped below the horizon, the gang crawled stealthily along the forest's edge, entering the dark passage that led to the treasury.

Meanwhile, Bhushan entered the meal room where food was being prepared for the guards who protected the treasure chamber. Ensuring no one was watching, he sprinkled a fine powder into the dish. Then, calling the cook over, he pointed to the top of the vessel. "The salt's not mixed well," he said, pretending to help. "Please stir it properly."

Embarrassed, the cook apologized and stirred the dish thoroughly, never suspecting Bhushan's sinister intentions.

Bhushan gave a friendly nod. "It's alright, just be careful next time."

The guards, unaware of the tampering, ate their dinner and soon fell into a deep sleep.

With the way clear, the thieves broke the lock with their tools and entered the treasure room, only to find it surprisingly empty.

They searched every corner, desperate for the riches Bhushan had promised, but found nothing of value.

"This isn't right," muttered their leader. "Something's off. Let's leave now."

Before they could escape, a loud thud echoed through the chamber. Kaal (Pranav) landed with immense force, his presence striking terror in their hearts. Moving with supernatural speed, he overpowered them one by one. The battle raged for nearly an hour, but Kaal emerged victorious. He tied the gang's hands with thick ropes and whistled sharply to summon the guards.

When King Mayanand arrived, the soldiers captured thieves and they confessed everything about how Bhushan had orchestrated the theft, supplied them with insider information, and drugged the guards. The cook later confirmed Bhushan's suspicious actions in the meal room.

Enraged, King Mayanand immediately ordered Bhushan's arrest. But by the time the guards reached his house, he had already vanished.

The thieves were summoned in the court for attempted robbery, and they confessed to everything, saying that Bhushan told them to rob the treasury and take all the wealth and to snitch on Kaal that he planned the robbery. They were sentenced to rigorous imprisonment.

Kaal, disturbed and confused, paced back and forth. Why had Bhushan tried to frame him? Why such hatred, when he had done nothing but serve the kingdom with loyalty?

So lost was he in thought that he didn't notice Varna and King Mayanand approaching. When Varna softly called his name, he looked up, startled.

"You seem troubled," the king said. "But you need not worry. We will take care of everything."

"I still don't know who I am," Kaal replied, his voice heavy. "And now this betrayal… it only adds to the questions that torment me."

King Mayanand placed a hand on his shoulder. "You may not have answers yet, but you have our trust and our love. Rest now. Let your heart be still."

He turned to Varna. "Would you like to stay with him a while longer?"

She nodded. "Yes, Father."

The king left them alone, the shadows of the setting sun dancing gently around them. The storm was not over, but Kaal (Pranav) was not alone.

Why do bad things happen to me all the time? What wrong did I commit for the people to hate me and plan against me? Who am I?

He was muttering many more questions under his breath.

Varna gently took his hand and told him to trust his destiny, as we never know what might happen. Time has answers to everything, and Karma doesn't leave any bad deed behind. It hits back. Good people will not suffer for long. "Kaal, you are a good person. I trust you with all my heart". I will be on your side through thick and thin.

Kaal's heart grew heavy with emotion, and tears started to flow down his cheeks. Varna wiped his tears, and both of them sat there for a long time until Varna started to speak in a low and calm voice. It felt like a cool breeze after a cyclone.

***

Chapter 16

Varna gently placed her hand over Kaal's and spoke in a calm, reassuring voice. "I know what's troubling you," she said. "I truly believe you come from a royal lineage. Your demeanour, your thoughts, your values, everything about you reflects nobility. And your strength… it's clear you're a great warrior. Whoever tried to harm you must have seen you as a threat to their power."

Kaal gave a faint smile. "You say that as though you witnessed it all with your own eyes."

Varna smiled back. "I may not have seen your past, but I've seen enough in the present to believe it." It is not about royalty that matters, but the kindness in the heart is what matters most.

Kaal's smile faded. "Still, I can't wrap my head around what Bhushan tried to do. Why would he want to get rid of me? What was his real motive?"

Varna stood and motioned for him to join her. The two walked slowly through the garden, the sky glowing with soft pink and orange hues as the sun began to set. Birds chirped gently, and the cool breeze rustled the leaves.

"How did you know about the attempted theft?" Varna asked softly.

Kaal sighed. "It was the night before the robbery. I was in the deep forest again, searching and hoping for answers. That's when I overheard a group whispering about breaking into the royal treasury. I hid in the bushes and listened closely. Once they left, I went straight to Minister Mukund."

"What happened then?"

"Minister Mukund summoned the trusted aides. He didn't want to alert the King until he could confirm the situation. They followed my information and safely moved the treasures to an underground vault, sealing the passage so no one would suspect a thing."

Varna listened attentively as Kaal continued.

"Later, I told Minister Mukund I would stay back to catch the thieves. I asked for four armed guards to remain just outside, camouflaged with the surroundings, ready to respond to my signal. The Minister agreed.

I hid in the attic of the treasury and waited. When they arrived and saw the empty room, they were confused. That's when I struck. I overpowered them and tied them up. When I was sure it was safe, I whistled, and the guards came in. And afterwards, you know what happened. The thieves confessed everything in the royal court including Bhushan's involvement."

Kaal paused, looking into Varna's eyes. "But I still don't understand why Bhushan would go to such lengths."

Varna looked away and sighed. "Because he wanted to marry me."

Kaal froze. "He did?"

"Yes," she said quietly. "He proposed to me once, but I turned him down. I told him I didn't feel the same. He pretended to be fine with it and said I shouldn't take it seriously. He remained loyal to my father. Or so we thought."

Kaal clenched his fists. "So he saw me as the one who took you away from him."

Varna nodded. "He believed that if you were banished, I'd be vulnerable and emotionally broken. He thought he could swoop in as the saviour."

"I see it now," Kaal said bitterly. "He wanted to paint me as a criminal… a thief. He thought once I was gone, he could manipulate you into accepting him."

Varna took his hand. "But I never would have believed it. I know your heart, Kaal."

Overcome with emotion, Kaal pulled her into an embrace. Tears streamed down his face as he whispered, "I'll never betray you, Varna. I don't need to search for my past anymore. You are my present, and our future is all I care about now."

They stayed in each other's arms, speaking quietly about the life they hoped to build. Time slipped away unnoticed. When night fell, they returned to the palace, shared a warm meal, and bid each other goodnight. That night, Kaal slept peacefully for the first time in what felt like years. He no longer yearned for answers about his past. His heart was full, and his mind at rest.

Varna, too, fell into a deep, peaceful sleep. She promised herself she would never hurt him. He had no one else to rely on, and she would always be his strength. To her, Kaal was everything—strong, kind, noble, and true.

But far away in Indraprastha, darkness brewed.

Bhushan stood silently as Prince Mahi Varma hurled insults at him. The plan had failed. Pranav Varma was not only alive; he had become a hero.

"You're pathetic," Mahi Varma spat. "You had one job to get rid of someone who didn't even remember who he was. And yet, here we are."

Bhushan clenched his fists, enduring the humiliation, but finally, he snapped. "Enough!" he shouted. "I've taken all I can. If I'm a failure, what does that make you? You couldn't kill your brother even when everything was in your favour."

Gasps filled the chamber. Mahi Varma's face turned red with rage. "You dare insult me?" he growled, drawing his sword.

His close aides stepped in, stopping him. "Let him speak," Kuldeep said. "Both of you want the same thing. It is that Pranav Varma gone. Work together."

Silence followed. Mahi Varma slowly lowered his weapon. After a tense moment, he nodded.

"You're right. We need each other."

They struck a pact, an uneasy alliance forged by a common enemy. They stayed up late plotting their next move, minds poisoned with envy and ambition. The next morning, Mahi Varma revealed his plan.

Bhushan listened carefully, then gave a twisted smile. "It's brilliant. Just say the word, and I'll play my part."

Their eyes met in shared malice. The game was far from over.

***

Chapter 17

Kaal (Pranav) woke to the sound of chirping birds and the soft sunlight warming his face. Varna entered his room with a bright smile, carrying a glass of freshly squeezed orange juice.

"Good morning," she greeted cheerfully.

He took the glass and drank it eagerly. "This is the best juice I've ever had!"

Varna laughed. "It's because the oranges were perfect today."

Kaal shook his head playfully. "No, it's because it was made with your love. That's what made it taste divine."

They laughed heartily, sharing a warm bond before Varna excused herself so he could get ready for the day.

Later, Kaal stepped out for his daily duties, meeting the people of Mayavan and listening to their concerns, both personal and civic. He issued spot solutions, gave instructions to the officials, and ensured the well-being of his people.

While he was engaged in these duties, he noticed a man moving hurriedly through the crowd. Something about him seemed off. Kaal quietly followed. The trail led him into a familiar part of the forest, the very place where he had once been attacked and lost his memory.

Suddenly, memories came flooding back.

He remembered his identity - Prince Pranav Varma. He remembered the betrayal by his twin brother, Mahi Varma. He remembered his father, King Indra Varma. A surge of emotions overwhelmed him. He wanted to return to Mayavan immediately to tell King Mayanand and Varna the truth.

But he was interrupted by the slow clap of hands and a familiar voice.

He turned around and there stood Mahi Varma.

Rage and betrayal stormed through Pranav's heart, but he held his composure. "Leave," he said coldly.

Mahi Varma smirked. "Ah, dear brother. Alive after all. How disappointing." He stepped closer. "If you breathe a word of this to Father or anyone in Mayavan, they'll pay the price, starting with our father."

Pranav's heart clenched. So King Indra Varma knew nothing.

Sensing his brother's thoughts, Mahi continued, "I told Father you were on a royal tour gathering wisdom before your coronation. He believed every word. He's waiting to crown you, blissfully unaware of the truth."

Pranav reached for his sword, fury seething within him. But before he could strike, everything around him changed. He felt paralyzed, trapped in what felt like a transparent, unbreakable bubble.

Then, a man appeared from thin air.

"Meet Albus," Mahi said smugly. "The greatest sorcerer in the world. Undefeated. Unmatched."

Albus raised his wand and drew a fiery circle on the ground. Green flames flickered into a glowing yellow ring. The surrounding space shimmered and then vanished.

Mahi Varma bowed to Albus, his teacher, who taught him the magic and made him powerful. Albus assured Mahi Varma that he will now be free from the evil clutches of his brother Pranav Varma. Albus believed everything Mahi Varma told him about his brother. So, he helped Mahi Varma in every aspect to save himself from his brother Pranav unaware of the consequences.

Albus may be a great sorcerer, but, he failed to read Mahi Varma's mind as Mahi is very good in manipulating everyone.

"No one will find you," Albus said. "No one will hear you. This trap is eternal."

Mahi nodded in satisfaction. "Now, I shall become king. I'll marry Princess Varna. And once I have what I want… Bhushan will be of no use to me."

Pranav screamed, but no sound escaped the bubble. His voice, his very presence, was erased from the world.

Months Later, in Mayavan

Kaal's absence worried everyone. Rumours of foul play, especially involving Bhushan, circulated. King Mayanand dispatched his trusted aides to search every corner of Mayavan. Princess Varna, devastated, stopped eating properly and spent her days hoping for Kaal's safe return.

On a full moon night, a man arrived at Mayavan claiming to be Kaal-Pranav Varma.

It was Mahi Varma, perfectly imitating Kaal.

Before arriving, he had executed Bhushan, framing him for stealing Indra Prastha's secrets. King Indra Varma believed Mahi's lies about Bhushan and told him to meet his 'brother' as it has been so long since Pranav left as Mahi is the only person who knew the whereabouts of his twin brother.

Mayavan welcomed the man they believed to be their beloved Kaal. Mahi knew everything about secret passages, traditions, and relationships. Thanks to Bhushan's information before his death.

He met Acharya Gopala first and sought blessings, then went to King Mayanand.

"I am Prince Pranav Varma," he declared. "Son of King Indra Varma. I was attacked during a hunting trip and left for dead until Acharya Gopala found and healed me. That's when I was given the name Kaal."

He spun a tale of how he recently regained his memory after recognizing one of the robbers, went to Indraprastha to reunite with his father, and returned to Mayavan only after King Indra Varma recovered from illness.

Everyone believed him.

He visited Princess Varna next. Though his appearance and words were familiar, her heart didn't respond the way it did with Kaal. Something felt wrong.

"I'm not feeling well," she said, excusing herself.

Mahi left, confident in his deception.

Back in the Forest

Pranav Varma, trapped inside the invisible magical prison, fought despair. He vowed to stay strong for Varna, for King Mayanand, for his father King Indra Varma, and for all those he loved.

In Indraprastha (Flashback)

Before traveling to Mayavan, Mahi had lied to King Indra Varma. He claimed Pranav had sent word, asking his brother to accompany him on the final stretch of his journey.

King Indra Varma, overjoyed by the news that Pranav Varma is returning soon along with apparent transformation of his younger son, blessed him and said, "May good always triumph over evil."

Mahi wept fake tears and left, his plan in motion.

He was now in Mayavan, playing the role of Pranav Varma, with everyone fooled.

Everyone, except Princess Varna.

Unable to shake her doubts, she visited Acharya Gopala and confided in him.

He nodded slowly. "You are not alone in your doubts, Princess. I, too, suspect something is amiss."

He outlined a secret plan to uncover the truth, one that could save their kingdom from the impending danger cloaked in deception.

***

Chapter 18

Everything was going as per Mahi Varma's plan. He couldn't have been happier. He had earned his father's trust, manipulated King Mayanand, and successfully deceived everyone in Mayavan. However, he was slightly uneasy about Varna.

Her behaviour didn't align with what Bhushan had described. Mahi Varma reasoned that her distant demeanour might be due to her long separation from Pranav Varma, and thought that she might be upset and assumed she would soon return to normal.

But Princess Varna had already set Acharya Gopala's plan in motion to uncover the truth about the man claiming to be Kaal.

She approached her father, King Mayanand, and suggested it would be appropriate for someone from Mayavan to visit Indraprastha to speak with King Indra Varma about the impending wedding. It was tradition, after all, to formally finalize such alliances to avoid future disputes.

King Mayanand praised Varna's thoughtfulness, admitting that in the midst of preparations, it had slipped his mind. He decided that Acharya Gopala, being his guru and a man of great wisdom and diplomacy, would be the perfect envoy.

Varna then requested permission to accompany the Acharya, stating she wished to see her future kingdom and understand its people and customs.

Initially hesitant, King Mayanand relented, on the condition that Acharya Gopala approved. The two visited Pratham to seek his blessing, and the wise teacher, already aware of the true purpose of the visit, readily agreed. Varna was pleased; everything was unfolding according to their plan.

A few days later, Acharya Gopala, Varna, and a small retinue of attendants set off for Indraprastha. When Mahi Varma learned of their departure, he panicked. Fearing exposure, he left the palace immediately, hoping to intercept them. Taking a shortcut, he rode hard, questioning travellers along the way. Finally, he spotted the group, two palanquins traveling along the forest path.

He approached, breathless, and greeted Acharya Gopala.

"This is an unexpected journey," Mahi Varma said, trying to sound casual. "May I ask the reason?"

Acharya Gopala replied serenely, "It is our tradition to visit the groom's kingdom before finalizing wedding rituals. I was curious, though, you seemed anxious when you arrived. You were riding like a man being chased."

Mahi Varma stammered, "I—I just wanted to accompany you. To make sure you're comfortable in my kingdom."

The stammer didn't go unnoticed.

"You never stammered before," Acharya Gopala said, raising an eyebrow.

Mahi Varma quickly deflected, "It happens only when I'm tense."

Acharya Gopala pretended to accept the answer but grew more suspicious. Mahi Varma then tried to persuade them to return to Mayavan, citing tradition that the groom's father should come to the bride's kingdom instead.

But Acharya Gopala stood firm. "Our minds are set. We wish to meet King Indra Varma personally."

Frustrated, Mahi Varma turned to Varna, urging her to return.

"You promised," she said softly, staring into his eyes.

"Promised? What promise?" he asked, confused.

That was the final confirmation Varna needed. This was not her Kaal. There is no such promise made between them except for the bright future to be shared. He didn't remember the moments they had shared. Still, she maintained a composed smile.

"You promised to take me to your kingdom when you regained your memories," she said. "But it seems that promise is forgotten too."

Mahi Varma realized he couldn't prevent their journey now. He forced a smile and agreed to accompany them.

That night, they camped in the forest. Acharya Gopala handed Varna a small golden box. "This contains magical *kajal*, made from ghee and a sacred wick. It grants vision in the darkest night and beyond."

Varna applied the kajal. In the stillness of the night, she spotted Mahi Varma lurking outside her tent. Alarmed, she pretended to sleep and called out to her attendant for water. Mahi Varma quickly retreated.

By morning, the group resumed their journey. From her palanquin, Varna used the enchanted kajal to scan the surroundings. She prayed silently for Kaal's safety. Her heart ached with worry, and tears streamed down her face.

That evening, they halted again. A potion, secretly mixed into Mahi Varma's food, lulled him into a deep sleep.

Varna ventured out under the cover of night, guided by the enchanted kajal. Deep in the forest, she stumbled upon a glowing green circle, its flames flickering faintly. Inside, suspended in a magical bubble, was Kaal.

She rubbed her eyes in disbelief. It was truly him.

Rushing back, she fetched Acharya Gopala. When they returned, the Acharya recited ancient chants, and Kaal's voice became audible through the bubble.

He explained everything, how he had followed a suspicious man into the forest, regained his memories, and was ambushed by Mahi Varma and the sorcerer Albus. How he had been trapped inside this magical prison, rendered invisible and mute to the world.

"My real name is Pranav Varma," he said. "My twin brother, Mahi, always envied me. Instead of bettering himself, he plotted against me. He attacked me and left me for dead. After I recovered, I promised Varna that I would never leave her, but fate had other plans. I followed a man into the forest and walked straight into a trap."

Varna sobbed as she pressed her hand to the bubble. "I won't leave you again."

Acharya Gopala looked grave. "Our powers cannot break this spell. The princesses of Mayavan are bound to magic only in defence of the realm. But there may yet be hope…"

He paused, then whispered, "The TRIO."

Varna looked at him in confusion. She is in a state of despair that she isn't able to believe in anything, given the state Kaal is in.

Acharya Gopala's eyes gleamed. "When magic fails—*TRIO* always accomplishes the impossible."

***

Chapter 19

Acharya Gopala continued, "During the reign of Varna's great-grandfather, it was the TRIO who helped the kingdom overcome a grave danger. Again, during her grandfather's time, the TRIO returned to save Mayavan from a terrible disaster.

Now, the time has come once more. The lineage of the TRIO must rise to defend Mayavan from the threat it now faces. That is why the TRIO has always been protected, no matter the cost, because in times of great peril, they are the ones destined to safeguard our people. This is their sacred responsibility, passed down through generations."

Acharya Gopala secretly sent a message through one of his trusted confidants to King Mayanand, ensuring that no one noticed. In the message, he explained everything that had transpired, how the man claiming to be Kaal was an imposter who had trapped the real Kaal, Prince Pranav Varma, inside a magical bubble.

He warned the king to remain cautious and not raise any suspicion, as doing so might endanger Mayavan. The imposter was none other than Prince Pranav's twin brother, Mahi Varma, a heartless man who had once tried to kill his own brother to claim the throne. He further added that Mahi Varma is manipulative and can make anyone dance to his tunes until his needs are fulfilled and will get rid of them later.

Acharya also wrote that the time had come for the TRIO to return to Mayavan. Only they could defeat Mahi Varma and save the kingdom from the unimaginable destruction he was about to unleash. Acharya Gopala assured the king that he would guide them towards victory, and then retreat into deep penance.

Meanwhile, Albus, who was guarding Pranav Varma invisibly on Mahi Varma's request, landed in front of them and apologised for the grave mistake committed. He also told them that he believed whatever Mahi told him without giving it a thought, as he always believed that good must triumph over evil.

In an instant, Albus cut his throat out of guilt and fell at the feet of Acharya Gopala and muttered under his breath that Mahi Varma would face a grave defeat and would perish. Acharya Gopala felt sorry for him and cremated him and prayed for the liberation of his soul.

After receiving the letter from the messenger, King Mayanand read it with great care and urgency. He immediately summoned his trusted aides and informed them about the contents of Acharya Gopala's message. He instructed them to remain vigilant, observe their surroundings carefully, and ensure that no one, especially Mahi Varma, suspected anything unusual. The trusted aides pledged their loyalty, bowed before the king, and departed swiftly to carry out their assigned duties.

Meanwhile, deep in the forest where the royal procession had halted, Mahi Varma noticed Varna sitting alone beneath a tree, her eyes fixed sadly on an empty patch of land. He quickly realized she was staring at the very spot where Pranav Varma was trapped. Though he couldn't be sure what she had seen, he decided he couldn't take any risks. Without hesitation, he used his dark magic to transform her into a tiny rabbit, trapped her in a cage, and threw her inside the magic bubble. Varna, still overwhelmed with grief, didn't realize what was happening until it was too late. Before she could even react, she had been turned into a rabbit and imprisoned, thrown away into the magic bubble near Pranav by Mahi Varma, who hurried back to Mayavan.

Mahi Varma thought about Albus, but didn't give much thought to it, as he had other things to take care of. Acharya Gopala returned after giving proper cremation and performing rituals for Albus and he immediately understood what went wrong and he knew that it can be undone only by 'TRIO'. He assured Varna and Pranav and went on to save the people of Mayavan.

Varna, now a helpless rabbit, began hopping around restlessly inside the cage, silently praying for the TRIO to arrive and rescue them from the wicked clutches of Mahi Varma. She also prayed for the safety of her family and the people of Mayavan.

Meanwhile, Mahi Varma returned to Mayavan and went straight to King Mayanand's chambers. Bowing respectfully, he lied without hesitation claiming that Princess Varna had reached Indraprastha safely, had grown fond of the place, and wished to stay there for a few more days.

King Mayanand, though shocked and already knew what happened, found himself unable to take immediate action against the imposter. Fear for his kingdom's safety restrained him from punishing the one he now knew to be a dangerous threat.

Still hoping to retrieve the rest of the entourage, the king dispatched his most trusted soldiers to the last known location. But what they found there was horrifying, a bloodbath. Everyone who had accompanied Princess Varna had been brutally slaughtered. Not a single soul survived, and there was no trace of the princess.

Gripped by rage and helplessness, the returning soldiers laid the bloodied bodies before King Mayanand and recounted the horror they had witnessed. The forest clearing had been turned into a massacre by Mahi Varma.

King Mayanand, trembling with fury, could no longer contain himself. He immediately ordered Mahi Varma to be brought to court. When the imposter arrived, the king struck him with a whip and thundered, "Your crimes demand nothing less than death! Bring back Princess Varna and Prince Pranav Varma unharmed, or you shall suffer endlessly." Without delay, he ordered his guards to imprison and torture Mahi Varma until he revealed the truth.

As the guards stepped forward with iron chains, Mahi Varma let out a thunderous laugh that echoed through the court like a violent storm. The sound was so intense that courtiers clutched their ears; some even bled from them. The soldiers trying to restrain him collapsed in agony, their hands burning as though touched by fire. The rest of the court froze, paralyzed with fear.

King Mayanand, stunned by the chaos, drew his sword and began chanting a powerful incantation. He aimed it directly at Mahi Varma. But before the spell could strike, the blade froze mid-air, suspended by an invisible force.

In that moment, Mahi Varma shed his disguise and transformed into a towering figure cloaked in shadow. His long black robe flowed like smoke, and a sinister sceptre gleamed in his hand. With a flick of his wrist, he cast a spell, turning every person in the royal court into cold, lifeless statues except King Mayanand.

***

Mahi Varma told him that Mayanand's powers might have saved him for the day, but promised to make him his slave once he became powerful and took over Mayavan. "Live in grief and despair as your subjects are turned into lifeless statues and cry for your helplessness.

"I am going to destroy you one after another starting from you, your Acharya and all of your daughters and your family. Your future son in law and your daughter will remain trapped inside the magical bubble till their death without anyone noticing them and in a helpless state where no one can save them.... Trapped for life. The day is not far. Wait for witnessing all of it", said Mahi Varma, his voice echoing in all directions.

Without pause, he marched to Pratham, the sacred place and started performing his dark magic rituals where Acharya Gopala once lived in peace and harmony with his disciples and blessing as well as guiding the people of Mayavan.

Acharya Gopala went to Dhatri's palace to convey the ongoing situation and told her that he would be going into penance, assuring her that 'TRIO are on their way and that they had to be guided accordingly. He also told her to take care of their palaces and places under their control, as it might take some more time for Mahi Varma to conquer everything belonging to Mayavan as his first priority is to get Mayavan under control. He also assured that the guardians will save everything and not worry. He blessed her and went away.

There, standing in the sacred grounds, Mahi Varma made a chilling proclamation to the people of Mayavan.

"From this day forth," he declared, his voice echoing unnaturally, "I shall dwell here until I become the King of Mayavan and Indraprastha alike. No one shall dare travel to Indraprastha to reveal the truth, for I will annihilate them or turn them to stone with a glance."

He raised his sceptre once more, casting it high into the air. It spun, then drew a glowing circle around Mayavan, a barrier of cursed fire. "Cross this," he warned with a cruel laugh, "and you shall burn to ashes."

Then he added with a wicked smile, "You shall all address me as *Kaal*—the embodiment of darkness, for that name reflects my true nature."

A wave of terror swept through Mayavan. People clutched one another in silence, too afraid to speak, for there was no one left to protect them now.

Unbeknownst to all, a small boy named Bopanna had been perched high in a tree on the outskirts of the kingdom, trying to pluck some ripe fruit. Hidden by thick foliage, he had remained unnoticed, protected, it seemed, by the very tree he climbed.

From his vantage point, Bopanna had heard everything. Frozen with fear, he waited until the dark figure vanished and silence returned to the forest. Then, cautiously, he descended the tree. But as he tried to step back into Mayavan, he was met by the flaming barrier—fire with gaping jaws that surged to devour him.

Bopanna stumbled back in horror, tears streaming down his cheeks. But in that moment of fear, something stirred within him. He wiped his tears and whispered fiercely, "I am the child of Mayavan. I believe in good, and I will protect my kingdom from this evil."

With newfound resolve, he turned and ran. His tiny feet carried him through dense woods and narrow paths until he reached the palace of Princess Dhatri. There, gasping for breath, he told her everything he had seen.

Her sisters Neeli, Rosa, and Aruni were there too, gathered for their monthly tradition of sharing a meal with their parents and sister Varna. But instead of celebration, they were numbed with the pain about everything Acharya told her, and Bopanna's words brought silence and dread.

A few hours later, a grievously injured soldier from Mayavan arrived at Princess Dhatri's palace. His clothes were torn, his body covered in blood and soot. He collapsed at the palace gates and was rushed inside by the guards.

Struggling to speak, he recounted the horror he had witnessed: how the entire royal court of Mayanand had been turned to stone, how many brave soldiers had perished in battle, and how dark forces now patrolled Mayavan, making it impossible for anyone to enter or escape.

"I… I played dead," he gasped, "and crawled through the shadows… I alone survived." A servant quickly offered him water. After a few painful gulps and a fit of coughing, the soldier steadied his breath and continued.

"Acharya Gopala has gone into penance… Princess Varna is missing… and Prince Pranav Varma…. he's alive, but trapped in a magical bubble. His twin brother, Mahi Varma, did this. He deceived us all. Acharya Gopala said… the time has come for the TRIO."

The princesses exchanged bewildered looks, struggling to grasp the weight of what they were hearing.

The soldier tried to continue, but his voice faltered. He fell unconscious mid-sentence.

Dhatri quickly ordered her attendants, "Lay him on the bed and call the royal physician at once!"

Dhatri and her sisters were overwhelmed by the grim revelations. Unsure of their next move, they resolved to act swiftly to save Mayavan from Mahi Varma's evil grip.

Together, they summoned the royal advisors to discuss their options and seek guidance. Among them was an elderly sage, the keeper of Mayavan's ancient lore. With a solemn expression, he began to explain the origins of the TRIO:

"The TRIO lineage is deeply rooted in Mayavan's history," the sage said, his voice trembling with the weight of memory. "They are descendants of families who once served the royal household with unwavering loyalty. Guardians of the realm, the TRIO carried out their duties with unparalleled devotion, shielding Mayavan from both internal strife and external threats."

He paused, his eyes scanning the worried faces of the princesses. "Centuries ago, the TRIO were sent beyond Mayavan's borders, tasked with immersing themselves in the outside world. This strategy allowed them to monitor potential dangers and defend Mayavan against invaders. Over generations, they mingled with outsiders, blending into their surroundings while keeping their mission alive in secret."

The sisters listened in awe as the sage concluded, "The TRIO were only summoned during times of great peril, when all else had failed. They can be contacted through an ancient medium, a channel that communicates directly with their lineage. That medium remains hidden, awaiting the moment it is needed most." The Princesses were already aware of the 'TRIO' and the sage's words only strengthened it.

It was time to summon the TRIO and awaken the ancient medium hidden deep within the forest. This sacred channel took the form of a golden, radiant peacock buried at the edge of the woods, in the garden of Rudra's house.

One peaceful morning, as Veena strolled through the garden, something caught her attention. A faint shimmer pulsed beneath the earth, tiny signals glowing and vanishing like whispers in the wind. Only those with Mayavan blood could perceive them, for they were invisible to ordinary eyes.

Veena froze. Her instincts stirred. Something was terribly wrong. These signals hadn't appeared for many years until now. She knew what they meant: Mayavan is in danger. The time for TRIO had come.

Wasting no time, Veena communicated to her closest friend, Samira, and told her everything she had witnessed. Samira, understanding the gravity of the moment, passed the message on to her father. The call to action had begun.

***

Chapter 20

Acharya Gopala opened his eyes and smiled warmly upon seeing the TRIO standing before him. "I knew you would come," he said. "Though I couldn't control every situation, I always ensured you were safe."

The children bowed respectfully and touched his feet. He blessed them, saying, "May you be victorious. Good always triumphs over evil."

He then led them to a well and asked them to fetch water. The children, unaccustomed to such tasks, hesitated. Rudra, however, gathered some tall, dried grass and twisted it into a rope with the help of his friends. Once the rope was sturdy, he tied it to a small mud pot nearby, lowered it carefully into the well, and drew it up full of water, handing it to Acharya Gopala.

Acharya Gopala took the pot and passed it back to them. "Now, share this water equally," he instructed.

Ansh took a sip first. The water was so sweet that he drank more than his share without thinking. When he realized this, he felt ashamed.

Acharya Gopala smiled gently. "Do not worry," he said. To their amazement, the pot began to refill itself to the brim. "It's a magical pot," he explained, handing it to Rudra, who drank his share and passed it to Aadya.

"This lesson is simple," Acharya Gopala said. "Listen carefully. Even the smallest task has purpose. Nothing is small and everything around us teaches us very important life lessons. Follow instructions with awareness and respect."

Every living being has a purpose and a task to be fulfilled. We must always search from within and complete it. Nothing can be compared as everything is different and unique with it's own purpose. We have to identify our strengths and proceed accordingly. You are your own teacher and choose your path wisely to fulfil your mission Donot let anything come between your vision and mission. Stay strong and stay united.

He then gathered the TRIO and began their training. "Before learning to fight the enemy, you must control yourselves—your thoughts, actions, and fears," he said. He advised the children to keep their senses under control and not to get carried away by their emotions and must always remember to stay united to defeat their enemy.

He stood on one leg, raised his arms in a wide circle, and began chanting. The children watched silently.

A radiant blue ball of fire, glowing with a silver-lined halo, appeared before them. Gopala opened his eyes and gestured to the children.

"Touch it," he said.

Rudra stepped forward and reached out. The moment his fingers met the glowing fire, he felt a surge of strength flow through him. The fireball vanished instantly.

Acharya Gopala turned towards them. "Power lies within you," he said. "But you must seek it through focus and discipline. I can guide you, but you must discover it for yourselves."

The children asked what they needed to do next. Acharya replied, "You'll learn in time. You are Guardians.... guardians born to protect Mayavan in its darkest hour."

He then told them to rest, as their real journey would begin soon. He called an attendant, who led them to their rooms, where they were served fresh forest fruits and a delicious tapioca root soup. They complemented the meal with refreshing mango lassi and sat together, reflecting on the day.

Aadya turned to Rudra. "What do you think about everything that happened today?" she asked.

Rudra replied in a thoughtful tone, "At first, I was excited. But now I realize the weight of who we are. People call us TRIO because we were destined to complete this mission together. I've learned that unity matters more than anything. We must not let differences divide us."

Ansh and Aadya nodded in agreement. Suddenly, there was a knock at the door. Startled, they waited as Rama, Acharya Gopala's trusted disciple, opened it.

He bowed. "Please don't be alarmed," he said. "We have visitors."

To the children's astonishment, King Mayanand entered, followed by Acharya Gopala.

They bowed and touched Gopala's feet again. He smiled and gestured to the king. "It is time for you to meet the true leader, King Mayanand of Mayavan. A noble ruler who serves his people with love and without expectation. A warrior who will go to any lengths to protect his kingdom."

Aadya gasped. "Your Majesty! We thought you were turned into a statue by Kaal!"

The king nodded solemnly. "I have the grant to use my powers to shield myself from danger. I used it to protect a few of my people before Kaal unleashed chaos. After he left the palace, I created illusory statues of them and escaped to join Acharya Gopala."

Ansh asked, "But if you have such powers, couldn't you defeat Kaal?"

King Mayanand sighed. "Our magical abilities were intentionally limited by our ancestors. They feared future generations might misuse their powers. So we were trained only to protect, not to destroy." That is why Protectors of Mayavan were created. To save everyone from grave danger and restore peace and harmony.

Rudra stepped forward. "Then how can Mayavan be saved by us?"

The king placed a hand on Rudra's shoulder. "Only true Guardians can save Mayavan. Your ancestors were among them, selfless warriors trained in all forms of magic and tested for strength, loyalty, and integrity. From their line, the TRIO was born."

He looked at each of them in turn. "Rudra, you will lead your kind. Aadya, Ansh, you will stand beside him. Together, you will defeat Kaal and restore peace to Mayavan."

***

Chapter 21

The golden rays of the summer sun filtered through the dense forest canopy, casting soft dappled shadows on the training grounds. The TRIO—Rudra, Ansh, and Aadya were already assembled in Acharya Gopala's armoury, examining the array of ancient weapons laid before them in the armoury.

They turned at the sound of a familiar voice. Acharya Gopala stood in the doorway, his presence as calm and commanding as ever. The children bowed in unison and greeted him with reverence.

"Let's begin," said another voice from behind.

The children turned to find a new face, one that resembled Gopala in stature and serenity. It was Sumanth Acharya, son of Acharya Gopala. He greeted them warmly and led them to a vast banyan tree that stood like a guardian in the heart of the forest. Around its base, a low stone bench encircled the trunk, inviting them to rest beneath its shade.

As the children seated themselves, soothed by the breeze and stillness of the place, Sumanth Acharya instructed, "Close your eyes. Let your senses guide you."

The TRIO obeyed, drawing in deep breaths, slowly bringing their minds into focus. When they opened their eyes again, the world around them had fallen into a strange, serene silence. Even the wind had stilled, as though nature itself held its breath.

Rudra spoke first, his voice low and uneasy. "I feel... watched. Something's not right."

Ansh scanned the surroundings with heightened senses, but found nothing. Aadya closed her eyes once more and then said with quiet certainty, "It's not Kaal. No one from his realm can breach this place. This is Suraksha, the heart of Mayavan's protection, created by Acharya Gopala himself. Here, we are safe."

Indeed, Suraksha was no ordinary place . Long ago, Acharya Gopala had embedded powerful protective spells into the earth itself, forming an invisible barrier no evil could cross. Yet, for years, many had doubted its purpose.

When whispers of its necessity began to spread among the people, King Mayanand had summoned the entire kingdom for a gathering in the royal square. Acharya Gopala stood before the crowd, his voice steady and filled with wisdom.

"There have been speculations," he said. "Let me clarify. Suraksha is not built out of fear; it is forged from foresight. Though Mayavan is peaceful today, darkness may come unexpectedly. Suraksha will be our last refuge when all else falls."

A villager had asked, "Why not protect the entire kingdom?"

"Power and magic don't work that way," Gopala replied. "But within Suraksha, I have poured every drop of strength I possess. When the time comes, this place will shield those who enter for protection and cast away evil."

And now, that prophecy had come true. Mayavan's people, once carefree, now roamed cautiously during daylight and returned to Suraksha by nightfall. Even then, many lives had been lost to Kaal's cruelty.

Rudra clenched his fists as he remembered those fallen. "Kaal will pay for this," he vowed.

"When do we begin?" he asked Sumanth Acharya.

Rudra, you are a born leader. Lead your kind to the path of success. Your leadership skills are natural, and you always lead your own kind with mutual respect and understanding. You are a person with no negativity and always calm. You have strong mental abilities which will be put into use when the time is right and needed, said Sumanth Acharya.

"The time is now," Sumanth replied. "But strength must be paired with wisdom. We must act wisely, not hastily."

Aadya added, "Patience is our weapon too. Rash moves will only empower him." Sumanth Acharya threw a sword towards her. She held it tactically without being hurt. You have a natural ability in fighting and handling swords. Let it come to use when needed.

Ansh nodded. "But we won't stop. He has caused enough pain." You are very good at remembering and analysing your surroundings and are a keen observer. Put your vision to good use.

Sumanth looked at them with pride. "Your training wasn't to make you warriors. It was to help you realize what already lies within. The TRIO was never made. You were born."

Aadya hesitated. "But… is it enough? What if our power still falls short?"

Sumanth gently shook his head. "You don't need more power. You need faith. In yourselves. In each other. The people of Mayavan already believe in you. Now you must believe, too."

He paused, then added, "Your motherland calls you. You carry her hopes, her pain, and her future. Protect her, not because of destiny, but because of love."

Silence followed—one that was not heavy, but sacred.

Rudra stood first. His voice rang clear in the still air. "Evil may rise, but good will always rise higher. We will fight not with hatred, but with purpose. Mayavan will be free again."

The TRIO stood together, hands joined, eyes fierce with resolve.

"We take this oath," Aadya whispered. "To destroy Kaal, to protect the people, and to restore peace."

Sumanth Acharya nodded solemnly. "Then go. Plan your mission well. This is not just a fight…..it is a promise."

The children looked at each other surprisingly with a lot of questions racing in their minds. Sumanth Acharya smiled warmly and assured them that he can understand what is going on in their minds and told them that they are born fighters and just needed to awaken their power which is buried deep inside them. Everything is perfect and that they must go on to accomplish their mission.

The children bowed and left, hearts racing with purpose. In the quiet of Suraksha, beneath the great banyan, the air stirred once more as if the forest itself had heard their vow.

***

Chapter 22

It was a bright, sunny morning when the *Trio* set out after seeking the blessings of Acharya Gopala and Sumanth Acharya before embarking on their mission to save Mayavan. As they walked slowly along the path, a sudden flash of lightning streaked across the sky. Startled, they closed their eyes; the brilliance was too sharp to endure, and they instinctively crouched to shield themselves.

Moments later, everything seemed to return to normal, and they resumed their journey. Still unsettled, Ansh asked about the lightning. "It felt like a camera flash mixed with a sharp lightning bolt," he said.

Rudra carefully scanned their surroundings for any clues, but none of them could make sense of what had happened.

Suddenly, Aadya noticed a large, shiny crystal lying on the ground, bathed in direct sunlight. The rays refracted into a spectrum of colours, creating an illusion of rainbow lightning bursting from the sky. She tried to lift the crystal, but it wouldn't budge. It was a naturally formed jewel, firmly embedded. Though there were many sparkling crystals scattered around, this one felt different—unique.

Leaving the mysterious site behind, they continued on their path, driven by their shared purpose: to save their forgotten homeland, Mayavan. After walking a while, they heard a loud thud behind them. Turning quickly, they caught a glimpse of a short figure darting away with the speed of the wind, vanishing almost instantly.

"We may have crossed Suraksha," Rudra said thoughtfully. "We're likely nearing Pratham—the cave of Acharya Gopala."

Ansh nodded. "What's our next move? We must be careful. Kaal is powerful… and dangerous."

Aadya interrupted, "Yes, we must stay cautious. But we must also not forget our own strength. We were trained by the greatest master of all, Acharya Gopala. We are destined to protect this land."

Rudra nodded in agreement, and they pressed on.

Suddenly, another loud thud echoed behind them. A cloud of dust engulfed everything, blinding them. They couldn't see each other, nor could they speak, unsure of what had just happened.

As the dust settled and the world around them cleared, Rudra and Aadya rubbed their eyes and looked around……. only to discover that Ansh was gone.

Panicked, they searched everywhere, but there was no sign of him. Then, from a distance, they heard the taunting voices of Akku and Tikku—Kaal's loyal followers echoing just enough to be heard.

Determined, Rudra clenched his fists. "We must keep going. We'll find Ansh," he said.

Aadya added, "We have to find him *and* save Mayavan."

"We will," Rudra replied. "The *Trio* will complete this mission—together."

Aadya smiled and nodded. They reached the base of Pratham, once a peaceful, sacred place. Memories flooded their minds.

Behind the cave, just as Sumanth Acharya had described, they found a narrow hidden passage.

Crawling carefully through the tunnel, they eventually emerged into a vast chamber. The room was enormous, with inscriptions carved into the rocky walls. Several other chambers and narrow corridors branched off into the unknown. To their surprise, torches on the walls burned brightly, as if freshly lit.

Rudra frowned. "Strange… No one has entered this place since Kaal took control of Pratham, and Kaal doesn't have access to this tunnel. Who could have lit these torches?"

He turned to Aadya. "Do you remember what Sumanth Acharya said about this passage? It reveals itself only to those with pure hearts and true guardians of Mayavan. Kaal, driven by cruelty, would never be able to find it."

They explored the adjoining rooms, searching for anything that might guide them. "I hope Ansh is alright," Aadya whispered.

"He is," Rudra assured her. "Kaal wouldn't harm him, not yet. He knows the consequences. He thought that Ansh is just a pawn meant to distract us. But we won't be shaken. We're strong enough to face him and save Mayavan."

In one room, they discovered a leather-bound book resting on a stone pedestal. As they looked up, a radiant light shone from the ceiling, illuminating the room in a warm, golden glow.

Rudra closed his eyes and suddenly felt as if he were drifting through the universe, passing galaxies and stars. He paused as he sensed familiar souls.... beings he couldn't quite identify.

When they opened the book, they found it filled with details of Mayavan's history. It's rulers, citizens, lands, and ancient events. Turning the pages, they were astonished to find beautifully painted portraits of themselves, labelled with shimmering letters: *The Trio.*

"This book holds the past, present, and future," said Rudra, amazed.

But Aadya cautioned him. "It's important to know our past and live in the present. But we must not make the mistake of uncovering the future. Some things are best left unknown. Let's experience it as it unfolds."

Rudra nodded. Yet, the absence of Ansh hung heavy between them. Despite their sorrow, they pressed on.

Rudra approached what looked like a wall, but sensed it was more than that, a concealed door. He slowly opened its latch, careful not to make a sound.

Meanwhile, Aadya took the opposite way which led to a closed door. She opened the door and found herself in a dense forest. The air smelled of rust and damp leaves. She listened to the rustling sounds as if searching for something irreplaceable. "Everything will be fine," she whispered. "We are destined to save Mayavan."

Elsewhere, Ansh slowly opened his eyes. The silence around him was unnerving—no voices, no footsteps. He scanned the area, missing nothing. Kaal laughed loudly, his voice echoing in all directions and warning Ansh not to try too hard to escape as his end is near and that his friends will also meet grave end after they find him and try to save him.

Kaal showered praises and compliments on Akku and Tikku for breaking TRIO as the mission willnot be accomplished further as it needs three to complete it and that he had discovered that the TRIO must be killed at the same time without even a gap of millisecond.

He further stated that the TRIO must be brought to the same place where guardians were once trained and the blow must be hard enough to kill them all at the same time. He went on boasting about his powers and how he destroyed everyone who came in his way. He told Ansh that his friends will definitely find him and that will be the end of TRIO and he will always praised for destroying the TRIO.

Ansh was quietly listening to all this continuous chatter and kept quiet so as not to enrage him further or to raise any suspicions. After this, Kaal felt that Ansh was threatened by everything and left to perform his dark ritual in the forest near Pratham.

Kaal stood in the forest , chanting ominously, his voice echoing through the cavern. Akku and Tikku scurried about, gathering ingredients like roots of henbane, dragon heart buried under the old banyan tree, magical rock reflecting three colours one at a time, and hair from a unicorn for a dark ritual meant to strengthen Kaal's powers against the *Trio*.

Back in Mayavan, King Mayanad, Acharya Gopala, and the entire kingdom were praying fervently for the *Trio*'s victory—to restore peace, and protect Princess Varna, their future queen, and Prince Pranav Varma. The thought alone brought tears to their eyes.

***

Chapter 23

"Focus, Aadya," she murmured to herself. "You will find what you are looking for. Don't give up." She closed her eyes, aligning her senses to one point. Time seemed to lose its meaning as she delved deeper into her focus.

When she opened her eyes, she felt more composed, determined, and resolute. A faint ray of light pierced through the dense, dark forest, beckoning her forward. She followed the light, finding herself in a place that seemed lost to time.

Taking cautious steps, she approached what appeared to be an enchanted boundary, a radium-lined circle pulsating with dark magic. It shimmered with an ominous aura, impenetrable and strong. Inside the barrier, Aadya could see a cute rabbit and Prince Pranav Varma trapped in a magical bubble, calm yet resolute, as if they were waiting for their chance to escape.

Aadya admired Princess Varna's bravery, reflected in her steady gaze. Despite being imprisoned, Varna's thoughts seemed to revolve around her people and the fate of Mayavan. Aadya bowed her head, offering silent respect to the royal pair. Using subtle hand gestures, she conveyed reassurance to them. Though no sound could penetrate the bubble, her message was clear: peace would be restored, and Kaal (Mahi Varma) would meet his end.

Steeling herself, Aadya resumed her journey. Shortly after , she overheard faint giggles and whispers. Quietly, she hid among the dense undergrowth bushes to eavesdrop.

"Mayavan will soon be ours," one voice said gleefully. "Kaal will enslave everyone and merge the lands of Mayavan and Indraprastha."

"Princess Varna and Prince Pranav Varma will remain trapped forever in that magical bubble," another voice added. "With King Indra Varma imprisoned, Kaal's rule will be unchallenged. No one can stop him now."

"Shhh! Don't make Kaal angry," the first voice cautioned. "The ritual must go perfectly, or we'll be in trouble!"

The two figures scurried off, their arms laden with items for Kaal's dark ritual.

Meanwhile, in another part of the forest in Pratham, Ansh chanted a few spells and carefully loosened his bindings. Rolling silently onto the ground, he retrieved a hidden scroll wrapped inside a series of boxes stacked precariously. Before he could open it, a familiar voice called out from behind him.

"Need some help?"

Ansh turned to see Rudra grinning at him. Relief washed over him, and the two embraced warmly.

"Rudra! How did you find me?"

Rudra explained that he and Aadya had split up after finding a secret passage in the magical cave. The passage, visible only to the TRIO, had led him straight to Ansh.

Ansh chuckled, "It seems our plan to let them 'kidnap' me worked perfectly. Kaal and his lackeys think we're broken apart. Their greed blinds them."

Rudra nodded. "Now comes the hard part: retrieving the weapon to destroy Kaal. Acharya Gopala's clues should guide us."

They recited the puzzle together:

"One that can heal the mind and a solid formed from a liquid state under pressure.

Found in nature, often in a cluster. Pure like a newborn baby, which will later grow into a beautiful thing one has never expected it to become.
A beautiful structure that grows slowly over time and can be found near or in caves."

Is it related to the stars? Ansh asked. Rudra smiled and nodded his head.

Or maybe related to computers, who knew Mayavan might be digitally forward, said Ansh playfully.

This is not the time to crack jokes, Ansh. Give it serious thought. We are running out of time. If Kaal finishes his rituals, he will become the most powerful beyond everything. We have to act fast.

Both of them thought through many options and couldn't come to any conclusion.

After some thought, Rudra exclaimed, "The crystal! The one we saw near Pratham!"

"Exactly," Ansh agreed. "We need to act fast before Kaal realizes what we're up to."

The duo navigated the secret passage back to the crystal. The sparkling gem clusters shimmered under the light, their beauty unmatched. They tried every tool they had to retrieve it, but the crystal remained firmly rooted.

Ansh paused, recalling another puzzle given by Acharya Gopala:

"I have rough skin, not smooth or sleek, providing shelter for those who seek.
Clothed in green and having roots nobody sees, reaching the sky but not trying to fly.
I drink from the ground, yet never drown."

Rudra's face lit up. "It's a tree! The tallest one!" This time, they didn't take much time to solve the riddle

Closing his eyes, Rudra activated his inner senses to locate the tree. He opened his eyes with newfound clarity and led Ansh to the spot. Among the towering trees, one stood taller and more majestic than the rest.

The two climbed the tree, searching its branches and trunk for a clue. Near the top, Ansh spotted an ancient inscription etched into the bark. Pressing against it, a hidden compartment opened, revealing a small, glistening key.

"This must be it!" Ansh exclaimed.

The key fit perfectly into a hidden slot at the crystal's base. As they turned it, the ground trembled, and the crystal detached itself, glowing with an otherworldly light. So, we need this crystal to detach the crystal needed to destroy Kaal, said Ansh, and we finally achieved it. Let's remove this and get out of here as fast as we can, said Ansh.

Back in the village of Suraksha, King Mayanand, Acharya Gopala, and the people of Mayavan gathered in the holy rituals praying for the Victory of TRIO and saving Mayavan. The place was filled with all the positive energy with the emerging chants. They placed their hopes in the TRIO, knowing that their destiny was intertwined with the fate of the kingdom.

"May the Guardians fulfil their mission," King Mayanand whispered, gazing at the horizon.

Ansh and Rudra, now armed with the crystal, set out to regroup with Aadya. Their journey was far from over, but their resolve had never been stronger. Together, they would face Kaal and restore peace to Mayavan.

***

Chapter 24

Aadya crept silently behind Akku and pulled out a small sachet of powder made with the help of a few students of Sumanth Acharya. TRIO learnt about different types of herbs and their uses. They learnt that nature created many herbs and plants which can save lives and few may be used to save themselves when in danger. when in danger.

Aadya, made the powder from a poisonous plant that induces unconsciousness and hallucinations. She held it gently under Akku's nose. Within seconds, he slumped to the ground with a soft thud onto the thick grass. Aadya quickly hid behind a dense bush, holding her breath.

Moments later, Tikku turned toward Akku, puzzled by his silence. As he approached, Aadya sprang from her hiding spot and struck him with the sharp knife she had earlier used to cut the henbane. Tikku collapsed beside his companion, both unconscious.

Meanwhile, Ansh and Rudra gathered their senses, attuning themselves to the surroundings. They noticed a faint radiant glow emanating from beneath a tree, just steps away. They knelt beside it, whispered a sacred chant, and Rudra reached out to retrieve the object.

It was exactly what they were looking for, a crystal identical to the one they needed to activate. Rudra gently placed it inside a protective box. Together, they headed toward the foothills of **Pratham**, where the original crystal was embedded.

Upon reaching the site, Aadya joined them and they opened the box and carefully placed the newly found crystal opposite the dormant one. The sun, as if sensing the significance of the moment, beamed brightly overhead. As the rays hit both crystals, a blinding reflection surged between them, glowing more intensely than ever before. The TRIO shielded their eyes, unable to look directly into the light.

Then, as the light subsided, a new crystal had formed—larger, purer, and glowing with otherworldly energy.

Far away, Kaal sensed the disturbance. His eyes widened in rage. He shouted for Akku and Tikku but was met with silence. Realizing something had gone wrong, he stood up, trembling with fury. Just then, the TRIO ambushed him.

Before Kaal could react, they tied his hands and legs and gagged his mouth, preventing him from uttering a single word. They placed the crystal on the ground and attempted to extract his soul into it, but nothing happened.

Kaal though bounded by TRIO could still show the malice in his eyes and wanted to destroy them. Ansh was little taken aback with Kaal's malice looks but was comforted by Rudra's gentle tap on his shoulder. Aadya said that everything is perfectly executed as per their plan and it is time to show the real villain Kaal his place.

She continued that however strong a person might be or whatever strength they might possess, evil intentions always leads to their destruction and their karma is always powerful which will pay them back.

Mahi Varma has done many awful and dangerous deeds that led to many people suffering and many even losing their lives which is why he has to pay a heavy price. The time must not be wasted as it might lead to further destruction.

Ansh has found new found strength with those words and he didn't want to waste any more second which might strengthen their enemy. As fear is anyone's worst enemy, he wanted to let it go and wanted to save his motherland. The three of them started to think of what needs to be done to destroy Kaal as the crystal is not destroying the Kaal.

Rudra suddenly remembered Acharya Gopala's words: *"Only when the TRIO unites as one force can Kaal be defeated."*

The three of them stood in a triangle around the crystal. They closed their eyes and merged their senses—three souls, one power. A radiant **third eye** manifested between them, glowing with the brightness of a hundred suns. Their combined energy surged through the eye and into the crystal.

The crystal began to pulsate, its glow intensifying.

Rudra placed it closer to Kaal. In a burst of light, it began to drain him, his powers, his energy, even his hatred. Kaal's body trembled as everything he once was, his strength, ambition, and magic was sucked into the radiant crystal. All that remained was a hollow shell.

Tears welled in Kaal's eyes as he realized what he had become. Powerless, broken, and alone. Rudra stepped forward.

"Your greed blinded you," he said. "You betrayed your family, your people, and your kingdom."

Ansh added, "You turned Mayavan into a land of fear. You underestimated us, thinking we were weak. Your ego destroyed you."

Aadya concluded, "You tried to kill your own brother, deceived your father, and destroyed everyone for power. There is no forgiveness for what you've done."

Kaal's body and soul were fully absorbed into the crystal. The glowing crystal fell to the ground with a dull thud, its light fading to that of a simple stone. Rudra picked it up and placed it carefully into the box, locking it tight and slipping it into his backpack.

They then tied Akku and Tikku with thick straw ropes and secured them to a tree to prevent any escape.

The TRIO rushed to the place where Princess Varna and Prince Pranav Varma had been imprisoned. To their relief, the magical lining had vanished. They were free. Varna transformed into her original form.

Varna and Pranav embraced, tears of gratitude in their eyes. "You saved us," Varna whispered to the TRIO.

The TRIO bowed deeply. "We did this for our motherland, Mayavan," Rudra said. "And for the people who deserve peace and love."

Varna's eyes glistened with emotion as she noticed the bracelet Rudra wore. She gently touched it. "I remember giving this to Veena. You are all deeply connected."

They returned to the palace together. King Mayanand, Queen Maya, and the entire royal family had gathered. Joy overflowed as long-lost sisters embraced, their tears flowing freely.

King Mayanand and Queen Maya embraced their children, finally reunited, their hearts full of peace and relief.

Hours passed as laughter and conversation filled the halls, but Prince Pranav stood alone, deep in thought. King Mayanand approached him and gently placed a hand on his shoulder.

Pranav turned, tears spilling from his eyes. "He was my twin… he tried to kill me and deceived my father. He even stooped low and imprisoned my beloved Varna and had the audacity to destroy you my king and take Mayavan under his control."

King Mayanand nodded solemnly. "It wasn't your fault. Mahi chose the path of destruction. You, my son, chose the path of righteousness. And for that, we are proud of you."

He embraced Pranav, holding him tightly. "We'll face whatever comes, together. We have each other and that's enough to rebuild."

***

Chapter 25

The sun rose over Mayavan with a golden glow that bathed the kingdom in warmth and light, an apt reflection of the joy that now filled its lands. At the palace gates, King Mayanand turned to the three young heroes standing before him—Rudra, Ansh, and Aadya, the legendary Guardians now known and celebrated as the *TRIO*.

With deep emotion, King Mayanand embraced each one. “You have done what generations feared might never be possible. You have saved Mayavan and restored hope to a land once cloaked in shadows.”

The children bowed low. Rudra spoke with humility, “Your Majesty, this was not only our mission, but our destiny. We were able to achieve this only because of our revered scholar, greatest teacher and noble being Acharya Gopala and we also progressed under the guidance of our beloved greatest guru, Sumanth Acharya.

As Guardians of Mayavan, we only did what we were born to do.”

Tears welled up in Dhatri’s eyes as she rushed to embrace them, followed closely by Neeli. “Thank you,” Dhatri said, her voice trembling. “For everything…… for your courage, your loyalty, and for giving us back the Mayavan we knew.”

Neeli added warmly, “And thank you for restoring peace and bringing back happiness. It means everything.”

Aadya smiled and turned to see Rosa and Aruni approaching. Rosa, ever exuberant, ran to hug them, while Aruni walked slowly, visibly transformed. Aadya stepped forward and gently placed her hand on Aruni’s shoulder. “Your heart is beautiful, Aruni. Promise me you’ll always stay true to your kind spirit.”

“I will,” Aruni whispered. “And I’m sorry for everything.”

As joy blossomed in every corner, Varna stepped forward, her hand tightly entwined with that of Prince Pranav Varma. He looked at the children with admiration and deep gratitude. "You have saved not only our lives but our future. Varna and I owe you everything."

His eyes lingered on Rudra, who quietly opened his backpack and retrieved the wooden box. "This," Rudra said solemnly, "contains the crystal. The one that sealed Kaal's fate."

Pranav took the box with reverence, holding it tightly. As he did, a flood of memories washed over him, memories of his twin, Mahi Varma. "Had he chosen the path of light, we could have shared the kingdoms… perhaps even ruled together, peacefully."

Rudra gently placed a hand on his arm. "You were the brother he needed, but not the one he deserved. You carry no blame."

Pranav nodded, tears falling silently. Just then, a voice called out from the palace entrance. "*TRIO always triumphs!*"

The three children turned in unison and ran into the arms of Sumanth Acharya, who stood with open arms and a wide smile. "You've exceeded every lesson, every expectation. I am proud beyond words."

"Where is Acharya Gopala?" Aadya asked, her eyes scanning hopefully.

Sumanth smiled. "Performing the sacred cleansing of Pratham. After what Kaal did there, the place must be purified. It will take a fortnight, and he could use a few extra hands."

With King Mayanand's permission, the children accompanied Sumanth Acharya to Pratham. The king announced that the ritual was of utmost importance and that no one should disturb the sacred work. He assured his people that the *TRIO* had brought lasting peace to Mayavan, and it would be completed with the ritual.

At Pratham, the children knelt and touched the feet of their revered guru. Acharya Gopala looked at them with pride. "From the moment I saw your eyes as children, I knew the spark within. My ancestors spoke of this day, and now you have fulfilled it."

Rudra replied with quiet reverence, "It was your faith that guided us, Acharya. Now we understand. You were always there, protecting us, watching over us, even when we didn't know."

The children stayed to help with the rituals by gathering herbs, chanting mantras, and preparing the sacred offerings. They returned to the palace only at night, greeted with warm meals and kind words. Their royal quarters shimmered with gold and silk, a stark contrast to the simplicity they had embraced during their mission.

Each day brought serenity. Statues of the cursed were restored to life. The streets buzzed once more with laughter. Children played, families reunited, and music of happiness returned to the air of Mayavan.

At the end of the fortnight, the entire kingdom gathered in the palace courtyard, where an announcement awaited them. Acharya Gopala stood tall and spoke with the gravity of history in his voice. "The time has come to unite Mayavan and Indraprastha through a bond stronger than any spell: Love."

The crowd erupted in applause as Princess Varna stepped forward, adorned in a shimmering silver saree and a golden veil depicting elegance and royalty. Beside her stood Pranav Varma, regal in his royalrobes.

King Indra Varma had arrived days earlier, humbled and regretful. He stepped onto the dais and addressed the people. "I owe you all an apology, for the pain caused by my son, Mahi Varma. I vow to honour the memory of those lost and to protect this land with my life."

Then came the grand coronation. Princess Varna was crowned *Queen Varna* in a ceremony filled with music, fireworks, and cheers. Soon after, Prince Pranav Varma was crowned *King Pranav Varma*, ruler of Indraprastha, his very own kingdom attended by everyone from Mayavan along with his own people in his kingdom.

Rudra, Ansh, and Aadya stood at the edge of the dais, resplendent in royal robes. Guests from across realms greeted them with awe, and they were honoured with medallions of eternal gratitude, forged from the kingdom's rarest ores.

Later, in their private quarters, the three Guardians sat on their gilded beds, gazing out at the starlit sky. "We did it," Aadya whispered. "We saved Mayavan."

"But we didn't just save it," said Ansh. "We gave it hope.."

Rudra smiled. "And we'll always be welcome here, guardians of the land."

As the kingdom rejoiced and music played late into the night, the *TRIO* knew that their story would be told for generations, not just as warriors, but as Guardians of peace, unity, and hope.

***

Chapter 26

The grand wedding between Queen Varna and King Pranav Varma was nothing short of a dream woven with love, triumph, and destiny. Nestled amid rolling hills and lush gardens, the venue sparkled with a mystical glow, as if the land itself was blessing the sacred union. The chateau-style estate stood tall and majestic, adorned with fragrant blooms and golden lanterns, echoing the grandeur of a fairy tale brought to life.

The interiors shimmered with warmth and celebration. Crystal chandeliers bathed the hall in golden light, while the sweet sound of laughter and soft string music filled the air. Every table gleamed with royal elegance, cascading floral arrangements, gold-rimmed china, and the gentle hum of happy guests immersed in the joy of the moment.

Queen Varna entered the ballroom like a vision from the stars. Her silk saree flowed around her like stardust, adorned with ancient hand-woven motifs and heirloom jewels passed down through generations. Her eyes held quiet determination and gentle vulnerability, a reflection of the journey that led her here. Her family, glowing with pride and affection, surrounded her with flower petals and whispered blessings.

King Pranav Varma stood at the altar, his calm demeanour hiding the storm of emotions in his heart. Clad in a finely embroidered sherwani and crowned with a resplendent turban, he looked like a prince from a legend. As Varna approached, their eyes met, and in that moment, every sorrow, every battle, and every hope came full circle. They were no longer just heirs to their thrones. They were the soulmates their people had prayed for.

The TRIO: Rudra, Ansh, and Aadya moved through the celebration, radiant in their royal attire. They smiled and laughed, but deep inside, their hearts swelled with overwhelming emotion.

They weren't just guests; they were the very thread that bound this joyous tapestry together.

The journey they endured, the dangers they faced, and the love they received had all led to this moment of serenity.

As vows were exchanged beneath a canopy of white wisteria, a golden beam of sunlight filtered through the leaves, casting an ethereal glow over the couple. It was as if the universe itself paused to honour their love. Tears glistened in many eyes. Some cried for the happiness of the union. Others, for the struggles overcome. And a few simply cried because this moment was too perfect to be real.

Nearby, two familiar figures watched the proceedings with pride - Acharya Gopala and Sumanth Acharya. Acharya Gopala's wise eyes held tears of joy, and Sumanth Acharya's gentle smile spoke volumes. The mentors who once guided the TRIO now stood silently, their legacy blooming before their eyes.

Later, Acharya Gopala called the TRIO to his side. "You have lived your truth," he said, voice calm and full of reverence. "You chose empathy over anger. That is the mark of true Guardians."

"You weren't just our students," added Sumanth Acharya, placing a reassuring hand on Rudra's shoulder. "You are our legacy."

Aadya's voice trembled with emotion. "We only walked the path you lit for us."

Gopala smiled. "Now the path ahead is yours to create."

And they would continue to walk beside future seekers, guarding the ancient teachings of Mayavan and preparing the next generation of Guardians. For the legacy of wisdom never ends. It only passes from hand to hand, heart to heart.

Farewell from Mayavan

The day of parting arrived like a soft ache in the hearts of all. The palace courtyard buzzed with heartfelt goodbyes. Dhatri and Neeli wrapped the TRIO in tearful hugs, refusing to let go. Aruni, her eyes shimmering with apology and admiration, slipped a delicate pendant around Aadya's neck.

Queen Varna and King Pranav Varma stepped forward, holding a beautifully carved box. Within lay three shimmering bottles glowing with a gentle golden light.

"These are pieces of Mayavan's soul," Varna whispered, her voice catching. "You no longer need doors to return. Just hold this, close your eyes, and remember who you are. Mayavan will answer."

Rudra tried to keep his composure, but a tear slipped down his cheek. Ansh held his bottle tightly, a symbol of love and belonging. Aadya hugged Varna, whispering a promise to return.

"You gave us courage when we had none," Ansh said softly, looking at the royal family. "You gave us purpose."

Rosa, with her usual warmth, kissed each of their foreheads. "Wherever you go, remember, Mayavan breathes because of you."

As their chariot pulled away, the people of Mayavan lined the streets, waving flowers and blessing them . And in that magical farewell, not one soul remained untouched.

Acharya Gopala and Sumanth Acharya stood silently at the palace gates, watching the chariot fade into the distance. Gopala's heart was full. "They were always destined," he whispered.

"And now they are legends," replied Sumanth Acharya.

A Hidden Truth

Back in Veena's cosy restaurant, the children sat together, sipping warm cocoa, their laughter tinged with nostalgia. Veena and Samira entered, sharing amused glances.

"Still talking about Mayavan?" Veena teased, ruffling Rudra's hair.

Ansh frowned. "But… we were gone so long. Summer should be over."

Samira grinned. "Time bends where love and magic meet. This is Mayavan."

In that moment, realization hit. Their adventures had unfolded in a realm where time danced to its own tune. The summer was still theirs. And so were the memories.

A Promise of Lifelong Friendship

Under the golden evening sky, Rudra turned to Ansh and Aadya. "I never thought I'd find a friendship like this," he said, voice trembling. "You both are my family now."

Aadya, now feeling elated as she has a big family, and with all the love and affection she is experiencing from Veena and Samira. She used to feel a little lost, and losing her family always bothered her. She is not alone anymore. She, along with Rudra and Ansh, destroyed Kaal, the evil one that killed her family.

Aadya is also happy that Ansh's grandparents always took care of her like their own. She couldn't ask for more. She wished that things stay that way always.

Aadya held their hands. "Let's promise each other something. That no matter where life takes us, we'll always find our way back to each other and to Mayavan."

Together, they raised their glowing bottles and made a silent vow. The air shimmered as if the stars above had heard them.

A Glimpse into the Future

Years passed, but their bond only grew stronger. Rudra became a renowned artist, his paintings of Mayavan inspiring generations.

Ansh pursued science, blending magic and logic to build bridges that looked magnificient.

Aadya, the storyteller, kept the flame alive in hearts young and old, reminding them that courage, love, and friendship were the greatest magic of all.

And Acharya Gopala and Sumanth Acharya - They became the stewards of legacy, guardians of knowledge, training new seekers in secret groves and hidden libraries. Their wisdom became legend, their names etched alongside the greatest ancient Scholars of Mayavan. Through scrolls, dreams, and whispered teachings, they prepared the world for the next TRIO, whenever destiny called.

And when the TRIO met, beneath familiar trees, among blooming gardens, under skies they once saved. They didn't need magic to feel whole. They had each other. Always.

Together, they stood, eyes fixed on the horizon. Hearts full. Spirits one.

Because once upon a time, they were just children. But now… they are legends.

THE END

AUTHOR-BIO

Hema Yanamala, an entrepreneur-turned-writer and former preschool founder, has always loved storytelling since childhood. With years of teaching experience and nurturing young minds, she brings warmth and creativity to her writing, inspired by her two children and supported by her ever-encouraging husband. When not writing, she enjoys cooking, listening to melodious music, and cherishing family moments.